Removing Blind Spots

FOR A LIMITLESS LIFE

DR. FIONA PYSZKA

Published, April 2023

Fiona Inc.

www.fionainc.com

717-917-8101

Unless otherwise identified, Bible quotations in this book are from the Amplified, Message (MSG) and the King James versions of the Bible.

All rights reserved. No part of this document may be reproduced or transmitted in any form or by any means, electronic, mechanical, photocopying, recording, or otherwise, without prior written permission of Fiona Inc.

Copyright © 2023 Dr. Fiona Pyszka
All rights reserved.
ISBN: 978-1-7369553-9-0

BLIND SPOTS

DEDICATION

I dedicate this book to my limitless family.

CONTENTS

ACKNOWLEDGMENTS

I am grateful for the amazing support of those that help me do what I do. My immediate family and my church family. Together we can do so much more. Thank you all for being a blessing to my life.

CHAPTER 1 – A WINNING LIFE

What does winning look like to you? Have you ever stopped to ask yourself that question? If we're not careful we can go through life only winning through battles waged against us, instead of intentionally setting our path to succeed. If you examine your life carefully, you may find that your success may be hinged on winning against a person, a system, or even negative thoughts. But, are these successes really winning at life, or are they just getting obstacles out of the way towards your own intended destination? These are questions that you should consider as you think about what a wining life would look like to you.

For the purposes of this book I would like you to consider a winning life as one that fulfills your intended purpose for being on earth. Which brings up another question that you should consider; Why am I on this earth? Many people consider this question and feel hopeless because they may not know why they are on this earth. Well, I am confident that why you are on the earth is possibly clearer than you realize. The first path to finding out your purpose is to understand that you were created on purpose. God, the Creator of mankind and all we see and cannot see, is the One Who sent you here on earth. He knew that He designed you well for such a time as this. Our design is not just the outward appearance of what we look like, but the inward gifting and capabilities of what we can accomplish.

A scientist and a painter may have two different skill sets in their ability to perform physically and maintain mental focus. Although their skillsets are different, they are both essential to being a part of what's needed in our current time on the planet. To decide that one is more valuable than the other would be ludicrous because each person is valuable because of whose likeness they were created. Genesis chapter 1 points us to the original design of mankind and the intended general purpose of man.

Genesis 1:26-27- AMPC - 26 God said, Let Us [Father, Son, and Holy Spirit] make mankind in Our image, after Our likeness, and let them have complete authority over the fish of the sea, the birds of the air, the [tame] beasts, and over all of the earth, and over everything that creeps upon the earth.
27 So God created man in His own image, in the image and likeness of God He created him; male and female He created them.

As we can see in these verses, God made us in His image and likeness. He also gave us authority over things on this earth. Note that He did not give us authority over people, but over the created things that are not in His image. Understanding the difference in our role between people and everything else created is a key to winning in life. God intended for us to control everything else that He created, except for people. The things under our control are supposed to listen to and obey us. We were given the authority for these created beings to obey us. Yet, Adam and Eve did not take their authority over the created serpent, and it cost them what they were given ownership of, the Garden of Eden and the earth.

Genesis 1:28 – AMPC - 28 And God blessed them and said to them, Be fruitful, multiply, and fill the earth, and subdue it [using all its vast resources in the service of God and man]; and have dominion over the fish of the sea, the birds of the air, and over every living creature that moves upon the earth.

According to God, man was given the authority to decide what happens to creatures in the air, in the water and on the earth. This is the authority that God put in our hands. The issue is that we end up giving that authority away with persuasion and manipulations of the enemy, Satan. The only one interested in derailing your life, and causing you to walk off the path of authority you were given is Satan. How does he accomplish derailing you? Simple, he deceives you. He is a deceiver of the brethren.

Revelation 12:10-11- KJV - 10 And I heard a loud voice saying in heaven, Now is come salvation, and strength, and the kingdom of our God, and the power of his Christ: for the accuser of our brethren is cast down, which accused them before our God day and night. 11 And they overcame him by the blood of the Lamb, and by the word of their testimony; and they loved not their lives unto the death.

The devil's accusation against mankind is constant and consistent. He has the same things to accuse a person of, even if the event happened one hundred years ago. The enemy will latch onto things because that is all he has on you. His deception is always based on something that you can or cannot do, and gives a reason to disobey God. We see that this is what he did with Eve in the Garden of Eden. He spoke to her about the tree that God gave her an instruction not to eat from (see Genesis 3). He did not talk to her about all of the trees she could eat from. He did not convince her to not eat from any of those trees, because she would not die if she didn't eat from the trees she was allowed to eat from. Her death was associated with disobedience to do something that God asked her not to do. Can you see the difference?

The devil will always tempt you to do what you were asked not to do, or to have you follow an instruction from him to do what you have the capability to do. For example, when the devil tempted Jesus to turn stones into bread, Jesus could have if He wanted to. He had the ability to do so, however, He did not turn rocks into bread. Ever wonder why? Because Jesus recognized the temptation. The temptation was not to quench His hunger, the temptation was to follow an instruction from the devil. Look at the whole account in Luke 4 you will see that during His time in the wilderness Jesus was being tempted by the devil. After He succeeded his forty days of fasting, the devil proceeded to tempt him. The first temptation would have been the easiest, which was to address Jesus' immediate need, food. But Jesus did not obey. The second and third temptations show us that the devil was not interested in Jesus eating food, he was interested in Jesus obeying his instructions. In order to derail your life, the devil just wants you to do something he tells you to do when he tells you to do it. But, even if there is something that you should do, you don't want to do that thing when the devil is giving you the suggestion. This is a key to not being deceived by the devil. Did Jesus end up eating after the devil left? Yes, the Bible tells us that angels came and ministered to Him. Jesus' food needs were met by God after the devil left.

How to Tell God's Instructions vs the Devil's

Let me share a story about my life and how I apply this principle. I serve as President for an orphanage organization in addition to my position as Executive Pastor alongside my husband, CEO of Fiona Inc. and Pyszka Consulting. In my position as President of the orphanage organization, I was bombarded with deficiencies in one of my staff living in residence at our overseas orphanage location. The barrage of accusations and urgency to do something about this person was unrelenting. However, I knew that acting on the information given, by the person giving it, was not the way that things should be handled. Although what the accuser was saying had some truth to it, I still knew that doing what they were asking me to do was the wrong decision. They wanted me to fire the person. Their intention of course (which they did not state) was so they could take over things. I did not do as they wished, and found out in the processes that the accuser was the same as the person being accused. A long story short, I not only did not listen to the accuser, but I also banned them from ever coming to the orphanage again. Sometime after, I had reason to, and fired the person that was being accused of different infractions. Now, what is the difference in when I fired the person being accused versus when asked to fire them from their original accuser? The originator of the instruction to fire the employee was the difference. In one scenario I was being asked to fire the person because the intention of the accuser was to take over the orphanage. Whereas, when God asked me to fire the person, I was able to do it quickly and swiftly because of Who was asking me. Not only did God direct me to fire the person, but He also gave me the evidence needed in the natural to follow proper protocol. Now, the end results were the same, the person was fired. The difference though was where the instruction to fire the person came from.

Now after a move like this in my example above, the enemy would want to come and let you know that he told you so a long time ago. It's in these situations that you secure your belief system so that you will never follow the instruction of the devil, but only the leading of Holy Spirit. Being led by the Spirit of God is how you demonstrate your sonship (even for women) to God.

Romans 8:14- KJV - 14 For as many as are led by the Spirit of God, they are the sons of God.

Your winning in life is highly connected to the instructions you follow. Who has your allegiance of obedience? God or the devil? The spirit or the flesh? Do you act on situations because of immediate relief? Or do you behave in a way that you can say you are being led by the Spirit of God? This is why it is important to treat people utilizing the direction of Holy Spirit. The devil wants you to run your relationships by his direction, not the leading of Holy Spirit. Gossip, backbiting, and strife setting are all ways that the devil traps you to make decisions about people. There will always be evidence to show you that the decision you should make is the right decision for the situation. However, never forget this process that we see from Jesus. No matter the current need, your capabilities, or what the situation calls for (Jesus being hungry), you never provide action to an instruction from the enemy. The timing for the action must be determined by God. Jesus was able to eat, but He did not turn the stones into bread, God sent Angels to minister to Him. God had a different plan. God's ways are always higher than our ways. He wants us to participate in His ways, but we must trust Him. The devil will always come to you at your weakest point and pressure you to do things. When God ministered to Jesus at His weakest point, He didn't ask Him to do anything, He just sent angels to serve Him so He could be physically strong again.

Matthew 4:11- AMP - 11 Then the devil left Him; and angels came and ministered to Him [bringing Him food and serving Him].

If you have participated in following the instructions of the devil instead of Holy Spirit, then take a moment now to repent. This is a step where you just ask God to forgive you for listening to the devil creating circumstances to push you into decisions. Commit yourself to God today that you want to be led only by Holy Spirit, and that you're capable of doing this because you are a child of God. If you are reading this book and you are not born again, please go to the back of the book for guidance on how to become a son or daughter of God. Becoming a child of God is the only way to win on this earth. Every other way will lead you to a dead end. The only problem is, when you're in the way of being led by the devil, you think that you're winning. The truth is, you're not winning down this path, you're only being used for the great gifts and abilities God put inside of you.

God wants you to identify with who He created you to be on earth. His plans for you are not to harm you but to give you an expected end (see Jeremiah 29:11). After you have made things right with God, which should take you seconds or at most minutes, don't identify yourself with past sins anymore. If you do not identify with past sins, the devil cannot latch anything to you. You are now operating in a new kingdom process. You have disconnected from the enemy by becoming born again or repenting for any direction you've taken from him. You have moved from the kingdom of darkness (under Satan's control) to the kingdom of light (under God's leadership).

1 Peter 2:9 – KJV - 9 But ye are a chosen generation, a royal priesthood, an holy nation, a peculiar people; that ye should shew forth the praises of him who hath called you out of darkness into his marvellous light:

If you were born again before and still followed the enemy's instruction, then just repent for those actions. Now, turn your life into a total surrender to God's instructions and see what happens. I am telling you; this one move can turn you into a winner in life. You will win in every area of life without having to fight battles every day. Why? Because you will be walking the path God planned for you, walking this path is a win for your life, and those you were assigned to serve. Jesus walked a victorious path because He obeyed God in all things. He did not do anything that His Father did not want Him to do. His life reflected His obedience to God, and His sacrifice on the cross proved His complete commitment to obeying God.

If Jesus can obey God completely, so can we. It is the devil that tells you that you are incapable of obeying God completely in your life. He is the one that is hoping you mess up so you can hang out in his turf for a while. The damage he has planned for you is beyond what you could imagine. But the opposite is that God has plans for you that are to give you the winning edge as you walk this earth. God's plans for you are so high and so big that we cannot imagine them all, and stand in awe when we see them come to pass.

1 Corinthians 2:9 – AMP - 9 but just as it is written [in Scripture], "Things which the eye has not seen and the ear has not heard, And which have not entered the heart of man, All that God has prepared for those who love Him [who hold Him in affectionate reverence, who obey Him, and who gratefully recognize the benefits that He has bestowed]."

God's plans for your life are perfectly calibrated for the time in which you live. The enemy wants to cause you to walk out of alignment, he wants you to be out of order, he wants you to fail. God wants you to win. God can make you the winner. God can make you the head and not the tail. He can cause you to overcome and move on. God can do this. God is the one that creates winners. Every story in the Bible that shows people who followed the leading of the devil, also shows their major defeat. To name a few, King Saul, Judas, Ananias and Sapphira and the one-third of angels that followed Satan when he fell. None of these situations turned out well for those who followed the devil.

On the other hand, look at how well things turned out for Jesus, Paul, Peter, James, John, and you and I. God's leading in your life will always make you a winner. His leading is personalized just for you. He gives you instructions based on what He's put inside of you. He will never ask you to do something He knows you're incapable of doing or not mature enough to do. God knows you. He's the only One who truly knows you. Following God's direction is the best way to live a winning life.

Now, let's find out some of the strategies that can prevent you from fully hearing and following all that God has for you. In the next chapters, I will show you blind spots that can be hindering your full win, and extended growth in the things that God has designed for your accomplishment on earth. As we continue in this book, I want you to keep in mind that every single thing that God planned for you, has already been written in detail in a book (See Psalm 139:16). The great news is that when He sent you to the earth, it was the equivalent of hitting the "publish" button. You are a published book of God. Whether people choose to read the book (participate in who God created you to be), or leave it on the shelf, the content of God's book still stands and it is a bestseller all over the earth.

You are a winning page turner on this earth. A best of the best. A more than anyone has ever seen. This is who you are, someone just like Jesus, walking on this earth. Now, let's get your winning life optimized.

CHAPTER 2 – VISION

Humans have the capacity to have natural and imagined vision. A person can see what is right in front of them, and also project in their mind's eye a picture of what they would like in their future. Vision brings clarity to the world around us. As a matter of fact, the Bible shows us that without vision people perish (see Proverbs 29:18). Without the vision of eyesight, people experience blindness. Blindless occurs as a result of the interpretation of what is visually available to one's brain. The human eye was designed to transport images to the brain for interpretation of what is before them. If the eye is unable to send messages to the brain, then blindness results.

In this book we will be looking at the phenomenon of blind spots in one's life that closely resembles the blind spots of the human eye. Although the human eye is a phenomenal work of art by our Creator, there is a blind spot that is attributed to the lack of light passing through to nerve endings, thus blinding the brain from "seeing" what is in the "blind spot". Webster's dictionary defines a blind spot as:

1a -: the small circular area at the back of the retina where the optic nerve enters the eyeball and which is devoid of rods and cones and is not sensitive to light - called also optic disc

b - : a portion of a field that cannot be seen or inspected with available equipment

2 -: an area in which one fails to exercise judgment or discrimination

From this definition we can gather that a blind spot occurs because of the eye's insensitivity to light. A lack of seeing something that is present, and a lack of judgement in a specific area or subject matter can all be attributed to or called blind spots.

Imagine living your life with unknown blind spots. What could you be missing out on? What areas of your life could be better, if only you could see? What opportunities may be right in front of you, yet you don't have light on the matter? Looking at this area of blind spots we will examine potential areas in your life that may currently be mediocre or a failure because of blind spots you are experiencing.

There is hope. Unlike the human eye's blind spots, the human life's blind spots can be corrected. Once you discover areas of potential blind spots, all you need to do is apply the correct light to the subject, and the blindness will cease to exist. How exciting! The key to eliminating blind spots is to allow light to enter the environment of blindness. Once light enters, darkness (the blind spot) is exposed and what was hidden can now be seen.

As referenced earlier, the Bible shows us that without vision people perish. Perishing is a position of loss and in some cases not possibility of change. Based on the verse, it would seem that perishing would cease with the introduction of vision. Vision brings light, clarity and direction to a situation. When vision is missing, focus is almost obsolete. Imagine a group of people dropped off in the middle of a field. No one knows why they're there; they are not sure who dropped them off, and no instructions were given. Each person would most likely start focusing on whatever is right in front of them, they may look around and mumble to themselves, or outright announce their confusion. Either way, all of the people would respond differently and accomplish nothing worthwhile but wonder, and aimlessly wander around the space.

However, what if the same group of people were dropped in the same field, except this time they were given verbal and written instructions on the objective of their visit. Being given a vision of what is expected, their attitude and focus would immediately change. Now they not only have a reason for being there, but there may even be a reward for completing the mission in a timely manner. The difference in outcomes produced was related to the presence of vision.

The same can be said about your life. Are you wondering around life aimlessly wondering what you should be doing? Are you chatting with the people around you without any goal in mind. Just talking and hearing stories, but at the end of the day no one was helped, you do not feel accomplished and you certainly don't feel as if you have something to show for your efforts? The difference could be just getting a vision. Without a vision you are living with a lack of vision blind spot.

Vision's Blind Spot

When there is a blind spot in your vision, you have darkness in places where light should be shining. First, you do not have a focus on where you are going and why you are heading in that direction. It is the equivalent of getting in the car and going for a drive with no intended destination in mind. For a short while, you will feel as if you are free and just having a great time. You will have no pressures of getting somewhere by a certain time, or having any responsibilities to fulfill. However, in reality how long do you think you could keep up this type of activity without stopping? Eventually your car will need gas, you will need to stop and take a break, and surely you'll get tired of just sitting and driving.

Driving aimlessly may be fun for a day or even a few, but eventually you will have the urge to produce a plan on where you would like to go and what you would like to do. It's the same with your life without vision. You may enjoy not having anything to tie you down, or people to ask you what you're working on or where you see your life in the future, but eventually you will start to feel unfulfilled and unproductive. When these feelings come, many people start drowning themselves in dangerous behaviors or habits that can ruin their life and those around them. What's the issue? The issue is that you have a blind spot to your lack of vision. Your life's vision portfolio is dark. There is no light on the subject of who you are and where you should be going. You have a life size blind spot called *no vision.*

The Solution

There's a story in the Bible about a man named Nehemiah who rallied a group of people to rebuild a wall to protect themselves from outside attacks and continued deterioration of their environment. Before Nehemiah could accomplish the great feat of rebuilding a wall, he had to first have a vision. His vision is expressed in Nehemiah 2:5.

Nehemiah 2:5 – AMPC - 5 And I said to [him], If it pleases the king and if your servant has found favor in your sight, I ask that you will send me to Judah, to the city of my fathers' sepulchers, that I may rebuild it.

Nehemiah's vision was to rebuild the city of his father's sepulchers (where they were buried). The beginning of Nehemiah's story showed a man who got bad news about his homeland and sadness ensued. His employer (the king) saw him sad for the first time, and asked what was wrong and how he could solve the problem. Nehemiah inquired of the Lord and got a vision. His vision was to rebuild a broken down place. What actions do you take when you get sad news on a subject? Do you stay in the sad mode, or do you inquire of God for vision towards a solution? Nehemiah did not allow himself to stay in a dark place, he inquired of God, Who gave him a vision of what to do. God gave him light to fix a dark problem. Staying in the problem mode will block light from coming to you. Wherever you do not allow light to enter, you are dwelling in a blind spot zone. Blind spot zones cause things around you to become unavailable because you cannot see them, or their use to you.

If Nehemiah were living in a blind spot zone, he would not have had an answer for the king's request to help. He would have preferred the king console him in his time of distress. The results of a king's consoling are only for a moment, but the problem will still persist because no vision for a solution was developed. Nehemiah's vision of rebuilding his home city started with the wall and if you read his story, you will see what the oppositions had to say, and how he responded. Nehemiah did not let the opposition deter him from the vision he laid out before he got to Judah.

Instead, he was able to have wisdom and strategy on how to handle the situation.

When you have a blind spot in the area of vision, you are generally at a loss for solutions. You feel as though no one can help the situation and there is no solution. The reason a visionless life feels as if there is no solution, is because there is no vision and the law of vision is that where there is none, perishing is inevitable.

Proverbs 29:18 – KJV - 18 Where there is no vision, the people perish: but he that keepeth the law, happy is he.

Your vision must have a revelation of God and His Word on the subject for which you are seeking vision. God's Word is the catalyst to creating the future you desire. Nehemiah desired to have a rebuilt city. He had not yet seen the state in which the city was in, he just heard about its demise. When he heard about it, he wanted to solve the problem. But he needed a vision to take with him to the city when he traveled back home. In Nehemiah's story even though he had vision, he met with opposition that wanted to kill the people for repairing their city. Imagine having a group of people who want you dead because you are rebuilding your house after a fire. This was a similar situation. Understand that the enemy of your life does not want you to succeed in anything.

He wants you to fail at everything you put your hands to do. But understand that God wants to protect you and see that you succeed in everything you do. If you understand this basic principle of how God sees us and how He wants us to live, it will give you so much vision for your future. You will no longer sit around and wonder if God loves you or if you should keep moving forward.

Instead, you will constantly seek God for the next level of terror to unleash against the enemy who wants to fight you and the vision that God has put in your heart. Here is what Nehemiah told the people when they were afraid of being attacked by the enemy.

Nehemiah 4:14 - (AMP) - 14 When I saw their fear, I stood and said to the nobles and officials and the rest of the people: "Do not be afraid of them; [confidently] remember the Lord who is great and awesome, and [with courage from Him] fight for your brothers, your sons, your daughters, your wives, and for your homes."

Nehemiah instilled vision into the people. He showed them who God is to them and reiterated the greatness and awesomeness of God. When the enemy attacks your vision, giving glory to God keeps you on track. It will keep your focus on where your help comes from, not where the problem lies.

Psalm 121:1-2 (AMP) - 121 I will lift up my eyes to the hills [of Jerusalem]— From where shall my help come? 2 - My help comes from the Lord, Who made heaven and earth.

Who are you working alongside in your life? Do you have a support system that has words in them to promote the vision God has for your life? Do you know where to find them? Are you not interested in being around people and letting them help you? All of these are questions to answer for yourself and honestly evaluate the gaps you may have in your lifestyle that could promote the enemy finding places to put darkness and leave you with blind spots.

You are a person that God has already designed a plan for, and your plan is custom made to suit your life and the gifts God has put inside of you. Spend some time in prayer and reflect on the goodness of God and the awesomeness of God. Then if there are any areas in your life where direction is unclear, ask God to give you vision. Maybe you need a general vision for your life, if so, ask God to point you in the right direction. You are valuable and needed on this earth. Let God show you why.

CHAPTER 3 – MIND TRUTH

Your vision can only go as far as you can see both in the natural and in the spiritual realm. In the natural, if you are driving down a road, you are only able to respond to what you see directly ahead of you. For example, if there is a vehicle broken down in the middle of the road one mile ahead of you, you may not be able to see it from where you are until the gap of one mile is closed. In the spirit realm your vision can be hindered not by distance but by darkness or lack of knowledge.

Knowledge is something that is processed through your mind. Your mind is connected to your soul. Your soul is the place where your life's activities are stored. The soul realm is where you feel things, where you store experiences in life, good and bad. It's the part of you that stores your connection to people and God. For example, in the Bible David describes what his soul knows about God.

Psalm 139:14 – AMP - 14 I will give thanks and praise to You, for I am fearfully and wonderfully made; Wonderful are Your works, And my soul knows it very well.

If your soul is shut off from God, you run the risk of

being internally tormented by the thoughts and memories you carry from life. So, if you had a bad childhood or a traumatizing experience in life, and you shut off people from your life, the only experiences you keep living life through is the trauma in your soul. If you shut God out of your life you are then shutting any input from God's Word to help the trauma you are experiencing. There may be things available to you in the Word of God, but you may not respond to it because you are shutting yourself off from the things of God. A person that shuts themselves off from God is generally unreceptive of what God is saying to them. For example, they may hear a message preached and think of everyone else that message could apply to but themselves. Or they may hear instructions from a person sent to them from God, and instead of listening to change, they listen to indicate that they already know what is being said to them. In other words, a person with an unteachable attitude will be closed off from hearing God. Many times people become unteachable because of pride or because they have been hurt too many times when they followed instructions. If this is you, understand that the correct instructions from people of God, will not lead you into disaster. Proper instructions followed could lead you into a promised land, just like the children of Israel were led to theirs.

How do you feed your soul good things? You renew your mind so that the mindset you developed through knowledge and experiences can be upgraded. What you feed your mind develops a mindset. A mindset can be compared to a thermostat. A thermostat is set to determine what temperate the room should be. One's mindset determines the level of thoughts you allow yourself to think, and the sources from where you are going to get new thoughts. Your mindset is also the limits that you have determined will be set on certain subjects in life. For example, if you have a mindset that someone who commits a horrific sin can never be forgiven, then you will not be able to accept someone as a new creation in Christ Jesus if they get born again. If you believe that you cannot become wise to a certain level of education because of a learning "disability", then you have put a limit on your learning abilities with your mindset of disability in learning.

There is a solution to change any mindset in life, whether society has decided our capabilities based on their scientific research and evidence, or we have picked things up from culture. The solution to changing a mindset is having a renewed mind. The Bible tells us to renew our mind continually, not just one time, but all the time.

Romans 12:2 KJV - 2 And be not conformed to this world: but be ye transformed by the renewing of your mind, that ye may prove what is that good, and acceptable, and perfect, will of God.

A renewed mind is necessary on a regular basis because we are constantly being bombarded with messages to reinforce the world's system in our life. In order for us to be conformed to the world, we have to be constantly reinforced with reasons why doing things the world's way will benefit us. We will never conform to something that we think will hurt us. The world has many enticing reasons for people to conform to its ways. For example, a person deciding that serving God is boring and there is nothing fun to do if you are a Christian. The world has determined what fun should look like. A certain type of feeling or "freedom" may be sold as fun, whereas the Christian lifestyle would be sold as boring. When in fact, the most fun a person can have in their life is to do the things that they were designed and created to do. If you are a musician, artist, businessperson, or parent, you may find many fun things to do in those environments and still be a Christian.

The devil knows that he may not be able to entice you to conform to the world, using worldly activities. So, he will use things that are part of our everyday lives. We all have varying relationships. It may be friends, families, co-workers, or peers, but they all involve people. The enemy knows that if you are not being persuaded through worldly things, he can bring conformity to you through relationships. Relationships will either increase or decrease the effectiveness of your life. Having healthy relationships is a secret to keeping a continually renewed mind. Good relationships share revelation from God's Word and not conformation to the world's system. You want to bring people close in your life that add to the system of heaven that you are following.

The Challenge

For the past twenty plus years I have conducted a woman's group at our church called WOVEN (women of victory enjoying newlife). When my husband and I first started pastoring the church (which we still do today), we had to establish some truths that were not known by the people. One of the truths that I worked with the women on was about proper friendships. I asked the women to conduct a test on their friendships concerning their conversations. Every time they spoke with their friends for about a week or two, they were to record how much of their conversation was about other people versus new ideas, or problems that they solved. The challenge was eventually to only speak about new ideas and dreams for the future or something learned from God's Word. They were to plan on eliminating talk of other people's business (gossip). What they discovered was that they had nothing to talk about if they did not talk about other people's business. Their friends (who were mostly not part of our women's group) would get upset with them if they changed the subject from gossiping about other people. What a revelation for the women when they realized that their friendships and long conversations with these women were fruitless. Nothing in their life changed for the best, instead, problems grew and became chronic instead of obsolete.

Why do relationships become so toxic, yet so enjoyable? Because there is wrong information in the mindset about friendships. Most people think that friendships are supposed to be supportive no matter what. But is that truth? We see Jesus treating friendship in a different way. When His friend Lazarus was sick and dying, He heard about it but did not drop everything to go to his aid. Instead, Jesus finished the assignment that God asked Him to do. When He was finished with His assignment from God, He proceeded to help His friend. Mary and Martha, Lazarus's sisters, did not quite understand this version of friendship and scolded Jesus for coming too late. But Jesus did not regret His decision, instead He did what He knew was possible to do, raise Lazarus from the dead.

John 11:5-7 - The Message - 5-7
Jesus loved Martha and her sister and
Lazarus, but oddly, when he heard
that Lazarus was sick, he stayed on
where he was for two more days. After
the two days, he said to his disciples,
"Let's go back to Judea."

Jesus helped His friend Lazarus be raised from the dead, but He also did it on His own terms, as led by His Father. This is key to friendships; you must obey God before you obey the request of a friend. A blind spot on friendships can derail your whole life. A friend can cause you to tread water in life, when you should be swimming ashore to greater things. A friend can also cause you to win battles and take territory even if it's just you and them. We see an example of a winning friendship in the story of Jonathan and David. Their friendship is recorded in the Bible.

> *1 Samuel 18:1 - The Message - 18 By the time David had finished reporting to Saul, Jonathan was deeply impressed with David—an immediate bond was forged between them. He became totally committed to David. From that point on he would be David's number-one advocate and friend.*

Read the story of the friendship between Jonathan and David in 1 Samuel 18. You will see how David's call was supported because of how Jonathan helped him. God called and anointed David to be king over His people. David's predecessor had been fired by God, and as a result he wanted to kill David. Jonathan was Saul's son, the technical heir to the throne in royalty. But he knew David was the man called by God and he supported David's position even against his own father, Saul. Now, that is the right kind of friendship to have in your life. Do you have friendships that would support your God given assignment? If the friends you have in your life will not participate in God's call for you, maybe they need to be looked at as an acquaintance and not an influential friend.

Renewing Your Mind

Until you have mastered the art of stopping ungodly thoughts from entering your mind in real time, you should create a plan to renew your mind. You need a plan to renew your mind or else blind spots will be developed and grow from your mind that will affect your life and may not be detected, if ever. Imagine going your whole life with blind spots that you grew in your mind and did not realize they were there. Maybe you're reading this book and already realize that you do have blind spots that you never realized were there. If you have already recognized this about you, that's great news. You are already renewing your mind in the area of blind spots.

There are several ways you can plan to renew your mind purposefully until it becomes a natural part of your daily routine. For example, write down words that you refuse to accept as part of your life. You can sit now and write those words, or keep an ongoing list as you hear things in your daily routine. For example, if you're listening to the radio and a song comes on talking about God, and their version of God paints Him as a thief, abuser, and out to get you kind of God, stop listening to the song. In that moment, turn off the song and say out loud, I believe God is always good and more importantly, He's always good to me. Make a list of who you think God is to you. You can even write down how many ways God has been good to you with real life examples of your own life. What you're doing is solidifying in your mind the good things that God does and has done for you. Your security in God being good will create a mind set in you that cannot be shaken about how good God is to people.

Another way to renew your mind, is to identify constant thoughts that magnify why you are unable to accomplish goals you have set for yourself. When thoughts come up that weakens your ability to succeed in any area of life, question those thoughts. For example, if you want to write a book, and when you think about writing a book, you think that you could never write a book because you are not good enough to write a book. Ask yourself, why are you not good enough? The answers you discover will let you know the thoughts that have been placed in your mindset to stop you from accomplishing the goal of writing a book.

By capturing thoughts that stop you, you will be removing any blind spots in your mind that may have remained because you thought they were from God. God would not stop you from doing something by telling you that you are not capable of doing said thing. God would ask you to stop doing what He wants you to stop. He gives you the choice to choose His instructions, or stay stuck in your own mindset. God would not steal your self-esteem and confidence to "get you to obey Him". Doing something that a thief would do is not how God operates because He is not a thief. A thief would steal time, money, health and wealth from you. God is not a thief, He would never steal these things from you, He would give these things to you. God is not an abuser; He does not give you something and then punish you because you were a bad child. He lets you keep what He gives you and He will teach you His ways of doing things better next time. When He teaches us through Holy Spirit (see John 14:26), it is our responsibility to listen and follow through with any instructions given so that we don't end up with a loss again.

If you accept loss, sickness, poverty, and strife as God's way of teaching you something, you have a blind spot in your mindset with the wrong image of God. God does not use the enemy to teach you things. He has assigned Holy Spirit to be our teacher. Holy Spirit is quite capable of showing us what we need to know and learn for our lives to be extremely successful and fulfilling. The enemy has no credibility on his own, so he has to use God's name to convince people, especially Christians, to terrorize them and make them think it's God. Because Christians want to please God, they allow these things to go unchecked in their life while they wait for God's big lesson to be revealed to them. If this is who you are, and how you think, I'm telling you right now, you MUST change your mind set about God's character and how He operates in a person's life. If you just look at John 3:16 you will see the basis for God's decisions concerning mankind.

John 3:16 – KJV - 16 For God so loved the world, that he gave his only begotten Son, that whosoever believeth in him should not perish, but have everlasting life.

In the first few words of John 3:16 we see God's motive for interacting with mankind, love. *God so loved that He gave* is the basis for how God operates. He loves us and He gives to us. God does not hate us and He does not take away from us. When we lose things, we must investigate and see why there is a loss. We should not automatically assume that the taking was from God. If we discover that the taking was from God, we should consider why it had to be taken. What you will see is that the thing may not have been given by God, it may have been a trap from the enemy. This is true in some cases in romantic relationships. Two people may fall madly in love and somehow had to breakup. They may be crying and very upset about the whole thing, but when inquiring from God they realize that they were never supposed to be together in the first place. These types of "losses" in our life turn out to be a God given gift to our future. Some people who are married now may wish that they had the opportunity to hear God tell them to not marry the person they did. Question yourself, why didn't God tell you? Did He try to tell you, through people, but you refused to listen? Ask yourself these hard questions, and answer them with the answers God gives you, not the ones the enemy provides through the mindset you have on the subject.

Your mind was created by God and should be the place that you consciously read and accept His Words, both written and revealed by Him. After His Word is accepted in your mind, then it can be stored in your heart.

Psalm 119:11 – AMP -11 - Your word I have treasured and stored in my heart, That I may not sin against You.

God's Word needs to be stored in your heart by you. Such storage is required for you not to sin against God. If you do not treasure God's Word to you, you are in jeopardy of sinning against God. He wants you to live a free, fulfilling life, and He has designed one for you. In His designed life for you, you win all the time. You win in every area, you are triumphant, and you do not allow the enemy to paint a picture of God that is not true. This is the life God has for you.

Why is it important to have the correct mindset of God? Because it is the foundation from which your identity can be built. If you have the wrong image of God in your mindset, you will automatically have the wrong image of yourself. How is this possible? In Genesis 1:26, the Bible shows us that when God was creating man, He created man in His own image, even though images of trees, animals, and the universe were present. God did not use any other image to create mankind. He used His own image and likeness. This means that we were designed to operate like God. God's motive of operation is love, and His action of operating is to give. God created a garden full of all that Adam and Eve would need without one request from them. He then gave them authority to name things that He created and gave man dominion over all that occupied the earth. God has put a high level of confidence in us to be able to handle what He has given to us. In order to accept and walk in what God has given to you, your mindset may need to be adjusted in God's goodness and His love qualities. God is the only one that is called love.

1 John 4:8 – (AMPC) - 8 He who does not love has not become acquainted with God [does not and never did know Him], for God is love.

Your enemy, the devil, has no love quality in him. He only has killing, stealing, and destroying in him (see John 10:10). Anything good that is killed, stolen or destroyed in your life was carried out by agents of your enemy. You were not born again to be subject to the enemy's plans anymore. You are a child of God and live according to the instructions that God has laid out for you. In order to fulfill the call of God on your life, you need to set your mind to accept and follow God's instructions without fear. This means that you will not be afraid that you're doing something wrong all the time. Instead, you will move with confidence and with the understanding that you know God's voice and you are capable of hearing Him when He calls to you. You must have your mindset adjusted to understand that Holy Spirit is your teacher and guide and He will lead you into all truth. You must understand that you have the ability to hear and know what God is saying to you, enough to hear Him tell you which way to go. But first, you must be going somewhere. Don't just sit around and wait on life to happen. Live, and live life more abundantly. Living is what God has planned for you. First you live on earth as a free person, then you live forever with Him. Amen!

CHAPTER 4 - PEOPLE

God's version of life on earth involves having relationships with people. In the Garden of Eden God created animals, birds, fish, and trees before He created Adam. After creating Adam, God realized that it was not good for man to be left as a single person. His realization was hinged on the concept of multiplication. God had commanded everything around Him that was created to multiply and keep multiplying. However, when it came to mankind (made in His image) He realized that Adam could not multiply himself without woman. Notice that Adam did not produce men and Eve did not produce women. They could not individually multiply themselves. Together they produced both male and female. In order for multiplication of humans to occur, two humans (male and female) had to be involved (see Genesis 2).

Before giving Adam the option of a wife, God brought other animals for Adam to choose a helper. But Adam found no one suitable to help him fulfill the multiplication God had planned for him to do. At this point in the beginning, God and Adam were working together on this project called Earth. God was setting Adam up for success. Until then, everything God created He stamped with a "good" approval stamp before leaving that created thing to multiply. However, when it came to man, God realized that leaving man to fend for himself in multiplying was not good. Following God's pattern of only good things to multiply, He created Eve from man's own flesh.

Genesis 2:21-22 – AMP -21 So the Lord God caused a deep sleep to fall upon Adam; and while he slept, He took one of his ribs and closed up the flesh at that place. 22 And the rib which the Lord God had taken from the man He made (fashioned, formed) into a woman, and He brought her and presented her to the man.

Adam was full of God's Spirit and was perfect. In his perfect state he made the perfect choice in accepting Eve as bone of his bone and flesh of his flesh and He named her woman.

Genesis 2:23-24 – AMP - 23 Then Adam said, "This is now bone of my bones, And flesh of my flesh; She shall be called Woman, Because she was taken out of Man."24 For this reason a man shall leave his father and his mother, and shall be joined to his wife; and they shall become one flesh.

Adam's recognition of the correct helper for him, shows us a key in how God intends for us to become productive on the earth. All throughout the Bible people did things for God's kingdom with the help of other people. The devil is keen on this principle too, so his people also had people who worked with them. What does this mean for you and me? It means that we need people to help us accomplish the multiplication factor that we are assigned to fulfill. The mandate to multiply does not only extend to the birth of other humans on the earth. It is the commissioning of humans to create an environment on earth where God can be glorified and His will be done like it is in heaven.

Matthew 6:9-10 – AMPC - 9 Pray, therefore, like this: Our Father Who is in heaven, hallowed (kept holy) be Your name. 10 Your kingdom come, Your will be done on earth as it is in heaven.

God would like us to enjoy the perfect environment of heaven, like He has on earth. Now, I understand that because sin exists on the earth, the exact environment of heaven is impossible right now. However, the perfect will of heaven can exist on earth. The perfect will for each of us can exist on earth. If this were not possible, Jesus would not have taught His disciples to pray for God's perfect will in heaven to be accomplished on earth. Jesus came to earth to show us what was possible. I think we can all agree that Jesus fulfilled the perfect will of God on earth for His life. Jesus did not miss a step, neither did He allow people or situations to block His accomplishing the will of God for His life on earth.

When Jesus came to earth, it was under very harsh rulership. If you read the accounts in the gospels of Jesus' birth and what took place right after, you will find the kinds of evil activity that occurred. Yet, God preserved Jesus through all of it. Jesus was protected by His parents before He could take care of Himself. Jesus was then helped by disciples that He chose when He walked into ministry. All of these people had a part to play in Jesus' fulfilling the perfect will of God for His life. Even at the age of twelve when He sat with the scribes and elders asking questions about their expertise in the laws of Moses, He was utilizing the help of people to follow the perfect will of God for His life.

All throughout the Old and New Testament, we see that when God asked someone to do something for Him, it required the aid of other people. Even if the aid was for a one-time event, or a lifetime commitment, people were still necessary. Why is this the way of God? We can ask Him someday when we see Him, ☺ but for now, we can work within the system He created for us to be successful.

The Blind Spot

God's system of working with people highly relies on the love principle of loving others as we love ourselves. If you can grasp the concept that people want to be loved and understood just like you would like to be, then you will understand how people operate. But if you have a lack of understanding on how people operate, you will have a blind spot about people. If you have a blind spot about people, you run the risk of being derailed from the perfect will of God for your life. We see it portrayed in movies or you may even know real life dramas where people have disagreements and families split, company break ups, and even church splits occur because of the lack of understanding between people. Today we have people identified as narcissists, multiple personalities, and other such issues that disables them from having healthy relationships with other people.

People boast about their ability to get along better with animals than people. God did not design you to have a better relationship with an animal than you should have with a fellow human. Thinking this way is a major blind spot and you can end up missing opportunities in your life because of the broken link of relationship with one person.

As powerful and anointed as Jesus was, His ministry team consisted of twelve disciples and multiple followers. He had people who financially supported Him and those who administratively supported Him. He had a treasurer and close companions that He took on ministry appointments. He had friends that He had dinner with and a mother and brothers that were known to His community.

Jesus maintained healthy relationships throughout His time on earth. What did those healthy relationships look like? When He was told that His best friend, Lazarus, was sick and He should come at once, He did not follow the pull of the need. Instead, Jesus continued doing the Father's will and then went to help His friend (see John 11). If your relationships are based on you neglecting God's service to fulfill the desire of a friend, then your priority of the love commandment has been compromised.

The love commandment asks that we put God first, and people are to be treated with the same priority as us (Mark 12:30-31). Putting God first means to put His requests of us first, then everything else can be given our attention. For example, let's say God asks you to stop what you are doing and make a phone call. As you're about to make the phone call, you get an emergency call from a friend or family member that requires your attention. What you should do is make the phone call and then attend to the emergency (if it requires you to go somewhere other than where you are). Of course, if you are right there and the family member is choking or requires CPR that's a different situation, use wisdom.

When dealing with people's issues and needs, you will find that sometimes your time and priorities are left for last, as people pull on you to fulfill their expectations of you. They may have a concept of the needs you're required to fulfill for them, but it may not be God's plan for your time. Just like Jesus gave priority of time to God's instructions, we must also do the same. The Bible shows us how to manage friends and relatives in our lives while doing God's will. Jesus lived a life with friendships and families and still accomplished God's will completely. His example gives us hope that we can also do the same.

When Jesus was told His mother and brother were there to see Him, He shared a teachable moment of understanding about who real mothers and brothers were (see Luke 8:20-22). Jesus kept His relationships solid by keeping people in their rightful place in reference to the will of God for His life. How could He manage to keep perspective and people in their rightful place concerning the will of God for Him? He walked in love. My friend if you want to develop solid relationships with people, you must develop your love walk. Not the type of manipulative love that involves doing favors for people so they would do favors for you, but the kind of love that comes from God.

The love that God talks about in John 3:16. The only person that can show you the depths of this type of love is Holy Spirit who was given to us to be our teacher. Ask Him to teach you the nuances of God's love and how you can operate in it fully. Read 1 Corinthians 13 and ask Holy Spirit to teach you what that verse means as you ready through it. He will teach you if you ask.

When you walk in love towards people, it doesn't matter what decision you have to make in the moment, failure will not be the result. We see the guarantee of love in 1 Corinthians.

1 Corinthians 13:8 – NKJV - 8 Love never fails. But whether there are prophecies, they will fail; whether there are tongues, they will cease; whether there is knowledge, it will vanish away.

We also know that God is love, and God cannot fail. So when we are walking in love, we are walking the way God would walk. God does not walk without love. Every action He takes is laced with the motive of love. It is clearly seen in a verse that most of mankind, saved or unsaved, knows.

John 3:16 – NKJV - 16 For God so loved the world that He gave His only begotten Son, that whoever believes in Him should not perish but have everlasting life.

God so loved; this is why Jesus came. Jesus did not come to prove to the devil that God is greater than the devil. God *is* greater than the devil and everything in the universe will testify to that fact. What God did in sending Jesus was to help mankind become in union with God again, like He originally created them to be before the infiltration of the devil. God was giving us, mankind, an opportunity to fully engage in who He created us to be. He was sending us a way to walk in His perfect will of complete authority on the earth again. God did everything for us. All of us. God loves people. God loves you.

Following our Creator's pattern gives us the protocol on how to treat people. God created everyone with free will and expects each person to make their own decision in life. As a result, we need to acknowledge God's free will in people and allow them to choose how they respond to us. We also have the free will to choose how to respond to them.

Here is how God allows people to use their free will: God presents a choice and allows people to choose what they would like to do. God respects their choice and keeps an open love offer for them so they have an opportunity to turn to Him, even at the last moments of their life. God does not close His love offer book from their access. They access God's love through receiving His offer based on His terms. His terms give preference and more benefits to the person than they could ever repay. Are you keeping records of what is owed to you by others with the plan to never speak to them again? The fact that God accepts someone into His Kingdom on their death bed, is proof that God is not into having a bunch of people accept Him on earth so that He could control them. No, God wants us to accept Jesus as Savior, so we can live without a slavery position with the devil. He wants us to have light in our everyday living, not the effects of death and darkness. God wants us to be free. We can only be free after we have accepted the salvation that Jesus' death, burial and resurrection offers. Jesus took our sins so we don't have to pay the slave owner, Satan, for our freedom.

God made having a relationship with Him easy. How easy is it for people to have a relationship with you? Although God has left the door open for people to come to Him if they want to at any time, He still expects them to enter a relationship with Him based on the parameters He establishes. We can have the same standard of relationship with people. Certain relationships have parameters that have to be met in order for them to be close to you, closer than an acquaintance. No matter what level of relationship you have with someone, you must still treat them with love. Remember, treating someone with love is simply not completely writing them off, but leaving the opportunity for them to repent if they choose to. Until their repentance though, you must keep yourself, your priorities with God, and your life safe from any harm they could cause. Someone that does not want to have a relationship with you, is not obligated to do so. Likewise, someone cannot compel you to have a relationship with them. I have advised many women over the years to remove themselves from abusive relationships. No one should be subject to being with people who abuse them. So, I want you to get a clear picture of how people should be treated when it comes to the love walk. Many people think that the love walk requires them to give everyone access at all times, no matter what. No, that is a blind spot generated by legalism and a lack of understanding of what the love of God was designed to do.

Test yourself today to see what blind spots you may have concerning relationships with people. Do they have to behave a certain way to be part of your circle? Can they be loud, quiet, educated, uneducated, rich, poor, male, female or any other criteria and still be acceptable in your life? People don't have to have a close relationship with you to experience the love of God through you. Jesus did not have everyone close to Him. Out of twelve disciples, three went to specific places with Him. Jesus qualified the access people had to Him, but when everyone (the big crowd) was around Him, they still felt loved.

Knowing where people fit into your life is a secret to walking in the love of God and fulfilling His will for your life. Everyone you know does not qualify to know everything God has asked you to do. The reason they don't qualify is not because they are not good enough, it is because they were not given the vision you were given. They may also not be equipped to support your vision with you. Understanding the position people should hold in your life is a key element to having blind spot free relationships with people.

Going it Alone

We just discussed the importance of having help in the calling of God for your life. However, there is a before factor. There is something you and only you can do before you receive help for the calling. You first have to accept the calling. If you don't accept the calling or an assignment, you have nothing that requires help. A blind spot is to have the wrong process of obeying God in your life. Let me explain.

When you are asked by God to do something for Him, He considers you qualified to answer His request. He is not looking for you to go and ask anyone for their opinion on the matter, or their input on whether or not you should accept God's instructions to you. This is a critical principle to understand in your relationship with God. The step that requires you to walk alone, is the step of saying "Yes" to God. Once you have said "Yes", then the resources and people will come. When those resources and people come, you are still in charge of utilizing their help in the proper way to fulfill the assignment you said "Yes" to God about. God is still looking at you as the owner of the assignment. When He is checking on the progress or looking for results concerning the matter, you are the person that will be evaluated. Jesus presented His finished work to God, indicating that He completed the mission He accepted from God.

Hebrews 9:14-15 – AMP - 14 how much more will the blood of Christ, who through the eternal [Holy] Spirit willingly offered Himself unblemished [that is, without moral or spiritual imperfection as a sacrifice] to God, cleanse your conscience from dead works and lifeless observances to serve the ever living God? 15 For this reason He is the Mediator and Negotiator of a new covenant [that is, an entirely new agreement uniting God and man], so that those who have been called [by God] may receive [the fulfillment of] the promised eternal inheritance, since a death has taken place [as the payment] which redeems them from the sins committed under the obsolete first covenant.

Jesus completed His assignment for salvation of mankind alone. There was a certain level of Jesus' assignment that He could not share the weight of with anyone else. It was Him and God working out the last details of the assignment Jesus accepted. Your assignments from God may require alone time with you and God while the assignment is being completed. What will you do then? Will you give up at the end because no one is coming along with you? If you think this way, you have a blind spot concerning your assignments from God.

If you remember Jesus' prayer time before the cross, where He sweat blood, He asked His disciples to pray with Him, but they fell asleep. They were unable to stand with Him during the most heart wrenching time He was having concerning being crucified. So much so, that He asked God if He could please take the cup from Him. But God did not answer Jesus, instead He sent Angels to strengthen Him. There is nowhere in the interaction of Jesus and The Father that indicated God answered Him with a comforting Word of support that what He was about to go through would not be hard on His flesh. But Jesus still carried on (see Luke

22:39-46).

A blind spot about doing God's will could be that we expect His will to feel good on the flesh. Rarely is your flesh going to enjoy doing something difficult. But your spirit will be joyful concerning what you're doing if you are doing it in the love of God. Jesus endured the cross for the joy that was set before Him. Jesus saw us when He accepted the assignment of the cross. Who do you see when you accept an assignment from God? Is there a blind spot in you where you only see the sacrifice you have to make, and not the potential of how others could be positively affected? Jesus said about the cross that it was joy that was set before Him.

> *Hebrews 12:2 – KJV - 2 Looking unto Jesus the author and finisher of our faith; who for the joy that was set before him endured the cross, despising the shame, and is set down at the right hand of the throne of God.*

Jesus did something that we should also do concerning assignments from God. Jesus despised the shame that dying on a cross brought. The enemy has setup a world system that identifies what is considered shameful and what is considered accolades worthy. The problem is that like with everything in the enemy's system, illusions are considered real and the real is considered shameful or not good enough. Loving God before yourself or others is not the way of the world system. Self-love is the acceptable standard, over love for anyone else. What the devil has not explained to his followers, is that selflove over love of God translates to disobedience to God. Love is a God thing; it is not a devil thing. But the devil wants to *use* love, the problem for him is that he can only pervert truthful things, he cannot obey them. Obedience to God is not an ability that the devil has. Only you have the ability to obey the things of God because God has shed His love in our hearts.

Romans 5:5 – KJV - 5 And hope maketh not ashamed; because the love of God is shed abroad in our hearts by the Holy Ghost which is given unto us.

Hope in God is what makes you not ashamed to operate in God's way of doing things. People without hope in God are more susceptible to walk in shame. Do you see how a blind spot of lack of hope in God can cause shame to become a part of your life's experiences? I want you to consider what assignments God has asked you to do that you may have declined. Now, think about the reason why you declined to answer God. Were you afraid of being a failure, or that you were not qualified (good enough), or don't have the time, or afraid of being mocked? Fine tune the reason down to the feeling you are avoiding – is it shame? Would you feel ashamed if failure happened instead of success? With what we have just discussed and realizing now that how you feel about an assignment from God is a blind spot, what is your answer to God now?

Take a moment and revisit assignments or instructions God has given you in the past that you may have ignored or said "No" to. Now, repent for your disobedience. Then, ask God which assignments He still wants you to do now. There are things in life that require proper timing, for that reason if we told God no, or did not hear God when He asked, we need to revisit whether or not we should still accomplish the assignment. God's timing is always perfect and we need to have respect for His sequence of events in our life. Our life's sequence affects activities in God's kingdom on the earth. Remember when the children of Israel first refused to take the promised land? They all thought they were grasshoppers trying to fight giants and they would fail. Only two spies representing two out of the twelve tribes thought it was possible to take the land. However, after the other ten tribes griped and complained about having to obey God in taking the land He had prepared for them, they changed their minds. But their change of mind was too late and out of order with God's protocol of how His Kingdom operates. They would not listen to Moses and their leaders, they decided on their own to go ahead and take the land after all. Everything about their behavior was out of order and rebellious. Yet, they insisted.

Deuteronomy 1:41-46 AMP - 41
"Then you answered and said to me,
'We have sinned against the Lord. We
will go up and fight, just as the Lord
our God has commanded us.' So you
equipped every man with weapons of
war, and regarded it as easy to go up
into the hill country. 42 But the Lord
said to me, 'Say to them, "Do not go
up and do not fight, for I am not
among you [because of your
rebellion]; otherwise you will be
[badly] defeated by your enemies."'
43 So I spoke to you, but you would
not listen. Instead you rebelled
against the command of the Lord, and
acted presumptuously and went up
into the hill country. 44 Then the

Amorites who lived in that hill country came out against you and chased you as bees do, and struck you down in Seir as far as Hormah. 45 And you returned and wept before the Lord; but the Lord would not listen to your voice nor pay attention to you. 46 So you stayed in Kadesh; many days you stayed there.

Do not have a blind spot of presumptuousness before God. If you had been given an instruction and disobeyed or complained about it, you must ask God again to show you if He still wants you to do that instruction. If you do not, then again you are being disobedient to God's plans. God's plans are not just about us individually, they are about the whole world. We have to respect God's ways and not just our ways. The children of Israel were defiant and rebellious and God could not work with them at the level He desired. Ask yourself the question, ask Holy Spirit to reveal to you whether or not you are easy for God to work with. Being a hard person to convince to follow instructions is not an easy person to work with. The blind spot that gives this hardness could be related to the identity you have of yourself. If your identity is tarnished and mixed with the devil's identity of you, then you will always question whether or not God meant you when He asked you to do something for Him. If you would like to find out more about your identity according to God's perspective, you can check out my book on the subject, *Identity Reset*.

Well, here's a beautiful wake up call for you. God always vets us before He asks us to do something for Him. It is His Name on the assignment, so He knows how to pick the people for the job. God already put everything inside of you that is required for assignments He has asked you to do, it's up to you to submit your obedience to the request. Here are a few people who obediently submitted to God without anyone else in their life being consulted:

- Mary the mother of Jesus (Luke 1). She said "Yes" to God to become pregnant. She never asked anyone's input to give an answer to God.
- Elizabeth, John the Baptist's mother (Luke 1). She did not consult anyone, including her husband, to agree with God's gift of a son to her.
- Hannah, Samuel's mother, accepted what the prophet Eli said to her without questioning or consulting anyone else. She also offered her son to God without consulting anyone else. Samuel became a great prophet of God where none of his words fell to the ground (1 Samuel 1).
- Moses, when God appeared to him in the wilderness at the burning bush. Moses did not consult anyone but did put conditions on God's arrangement with him. God allowed his conditions (Exodus 3).

Do some research for yourself and see what other stories you can find in the Bible. Understand that when God asks you for your "Yes", He does not put pressure on you for anyone else to give input unless they are also a part of the equation. Look at your life today, and examine whether or not the blind spot of always wanting other people's opinion before you can obey God is derailing your life's progress of success. If you find a blind spot in this area of your life, repent, and ask the light of God to flood the area so that you can see God for all His glory and power again. You can walk in the fullness of what God prepared for you before the foundations of the world, just by repentance and recalibrating areas of blind spots with the light of God. Now turn the light of God on in you, dance into your future with full victory.

CHAPTER 5 - TIME

A blind spot in the understanding of how time works will cause you to think that among all other humans, you are cursed with less time. The truth is that when God initiated the time command, He never changed it. We see the time commanded in the book of Genesis.

Genesis 1:4-5 – KJV - 4 And God saw the light, that it was good: and God divided the light from the darkness. 5 And God called the light Day, and the darkness he called Night. And the evening and the morning were the first day.

Before God announced the first day, good was announced about the light. God knew exactly how many hours mankind would have in a day to accomplish what was needed. He also knows how to stop time if needed so critical events can occur.

Joshua 10:12-14 – KJV - 12 Then spake Joshua to the Lord in the day when the Lord delivered up the Amorites before the children of Israel, and he said in the sight of Israel, Sun, stand thou still upon Gibeon; and thou, Moon, in the valley of Ajalon. 13 And the sun stood still, and the moon stayed, until the people had avenged themselves upon their enemies. . .

God knows how to make time work for His children. From this time on don't tie yourself to time, instead understand that every person on the planet has the same time. The difference between a royal child of God and a person who did not get reborn in God's Kingdom, is the authority we have over things created. Time is a created mechanism for man to function on earth. As children of the Most High God, we have the advantage of operating from a heavenly and an earthly realm. We understand that things in our life happen by faith because faith pleases God. As a child of God you should have a desire to please God. If you find a desire to please God is not in you, then ask Holy Spirit to show you why. You could be experiencing a blind spot against the character of God, from seeds planted by the enemy. Holy Spirit will reveal the truth about your lack of desire to please God.

Now back to time. The Bible shows us how things come into being on earth, they come from the unseen realm.

2 Corinthians 4:18 – KJV - 18 While we look not at the things which are seen, but at the things which are not seen: for the things which are seen are temporal; but the things which are not seen are eternal.

What is seen is subject to the law of time (temporal). However, what is not seen is eternal. Faith pulls from the unseen into the seen. Faith is a time hack for your life. Have you ever considered this thought? Let's explore the properties of faith and how it can control time.

People age based on time, and they have been told what their bodies can and cannot do based on elements of time. For example, it is understood that women have a child bearing age, and after that time she cannot carry a child in her womb. The difference between men and women for this timed event is different. Generally speaking men have a longer time to produce children than women. However, according to God's plans and purposes, He does not generally consider the time factor when He is ready to bring someone to the earth. We see examples both in the Old and New Testaments.

Genesis 21:1-2 – KJV - 21 And the Lord visited Sarah as he had said, and the Lord did unto Sarah as he had spoken. 2 For Sarah conceived, and bare Abraham a son in his old age, at the set time of which God had spoken to him.

In the story of Abraham and Sarah we see the defiance of man's use of time and physical abilities. God opened the womb of Sarah and brought to life the body of Abraham so that they could produce what people almost fifty years younger than them could produce. Mankind has learned to link events and possibilities with time. Time was never meant to be our master, it was meant to be a marker that we can use to document what we have done. In the book of Genesis, that's how God used time. After He created, He then announced the close of a day. God controlled time.

He did not indicate that He had one day to create certain things, He created and made sure the things He created were up to His standard. His standard is good. Until things are good, God did not move onto the next creation. Then after all of His Work God rested. He called the rest day the seventh day. During all of this creation and time moving on, God controlled things. He did not compromise and decide that things were good enough because He has to move on. No! God made sure things were good. What God created needed to last and continue to produce after their creation. As we see today, His work was good, because we are still benefiting today.

Examine your life, what things have you rushed through because you felt the need to rush so much that your work was compromised? I understand that we have things that require time, but again that's natural timing. God can make things happen through His miracle working power, that compresses time for your benefit. The New Testament shows the example of a process compressed into the time that was available for production.

John 2:10-11 – KJV -10 And saith unto him, Every man at the beginning doth set forth good wine; and when men have well drunk, then that which is worse: but thou hast kept the good wine until now. 11 This beginning of miracles did Jesus in Cana of Galilee, and manifested forth his glory; and his disciples believed on him.

Jesus' first miracle to start off His ministry was that of turning water into wine. The miracle was not just producing wine using only water, it was also that He took a process of years and compressed it to the time it took to fill up water pots and serve the first glass. Jesus Himself did not even do the work, He instructed the servants at the wedding on what to do. These servants were participating in a miracle of time and did not even realize that they were. Their obedience led to the operation of a process that in the natural would be impossible.

Another time compressed miracle that Jesus did was to turn five loaves and two fish into a feast for over five thousand people. We see the story in the Bible where Jesus demonstrated how to control time to accomplish what needed to be done. Jesus was teaching people who He saw looked like sheep without a shepherd. He was moved with compassion to teach them. But at the end of His teaching, the disciples made an observation to Him.

Mark 6:35-36 – AMP -35 When the day was nearly gone, His disciples came to Him and said, "This is an isolated place, and it is already late; 36 send the crowds away so that they may go into the surrounding countryside and villages and buy themselves something to eat."

Jesus's view of the people and the disciples' view were very different. The disciples were thinking in the limitation of time, whereas Jesus was thinking in the possibilities of love. Jesus was moved with compassion when He began His ministry to the people. Compassion is an element of showing care for people. Jesus was demonstrating His love for people through compassion. His compassion for them could not send them away hungry. The limitations of time did not hinder Jesus from fulfilling what was in His heart to do towards the large crowd of over five thousand people. Examine your own life. Would you have considered the time element like the disciples did? If you are thinking "Yes" I would, then identify this blind spot concerning time and fulfilling what God would like to show through you towards people. Jesus was demonstrating to these people what the compassion of God looks like. He did not allow time to run out before the full manifestation of God's compassion could be shown to them.

What areas of your life have you allowed time to dictate how much of God's plan can work through you? Have you already decided what you're able to do and not do based on time elements of age, ability, or season? The disciples determined that 'too late' in the day, was also 'too late' to help the crowd anymore. Do you have a blind spot on when helping should stop? Have you cut an assignment short or eliminated helping people in an area of life altogether because of time? Have you decided things will take too long, or that you don't have that kind of time to accomplish what God asked you to do? Or you may even think that what scripture says you should do as a believer is too time consuming for you to participate. These are some of the blind spots that can exist in people even though their heart's desire is to follow God.

My Time Story

In 2019 while in prayer, God revealed to me that I disobeyed an instruction from Him eighteen years prior. Wow, I was shocked and immediately asked for the instruction again. He showed me that He asked me to pursue my doctoral degree in business, but I never did. I was in shock and tried to remember when I would have heard and denied the request. No remembrance of the incidence came to mind, however, if God told me I did, then I did. So, the Lord asked me again to pursue my doctoral degree in business. My husband was out of the country at the time and when he called the same night, I alerted him that I would be starting my doctoral degree. That night I started researching where I could study for this degree. I started with the college I had just seen at another college orientation just prior. I filled out the application, tried to submit it three times, and it would not send. There were no errors on the page, it just wouldn't send. It was close to midnight at this point, and I knew that I was going to have a busy day the next day, so I wanted to get to sleep. However, before I did, I decided to search for colleges that have a doctoral degree in business. A list of schools came up and I started perusing their websites. I went to sleep without submitting an application.

That night in a dream, I saw all the information from the school I had filled out an application for, move from their page to the page of another college. The next day, I immediately transferred the information from the already filled out page to the one I saw in my dream. I also wanted to be sure that I was able to pay cash for my degree and not take out a loan. God worked it out for me to be able to do just that. I also wanted the degree to have hands on consulting with a business as my final thesis instead of just writing a theoretical research paper. The month I started my degree with the university, they announced that they are adding another option for doctoral candidates, a consulting project as their final thesis. Wow!

Fast forward to three and a half years later, 2022, I am ready to perform my consultation with a company that was vetted and approved by the school. I am in my last sixteen weeks of school and excited to finish and graduate. Eight weeks in, this company pulled out of the project. I tried everything I could to convince them to continue with me. They were not interested. I had only eight weeks left before graduation, as they pulled out in February and graduation is in May.

Time was a major issue in completing my final thesis. Now I had to find a new company, vet them, have them approved and start the consulting project from scratch, a process that happened over a one year period with the previous company. I prayed about God finding me the right company and I kept saying "I don't care what happens, I am graduating in May and I will be fully finished with my degree when I walk at the graduation ceremony".

Meanwhile, my doctoral chair was advising me that I may need to push my completion back another year. He assured me that many people take this additional time to complete their degrees, that it's normal. He also pointed out that I was doing my degree in record time, comparably speaking. Well, I refused to agree with the timing of the natural examples around me. I wanted to graduate. Here's the final result, I graduated in May of 2022, *on time.* Not only did I graduate on time, but I also had my completed work for the degree finished one week ahead of schedule. God literally helped me do in four weeks what would take a year to do. It took me four weeks to find another company to work with, which only left me with four weeks to complete the entire project. Folks, not only did I complete the consultation, but I solved the problem I set out to solve. Only God can help you accelerate things in your life. I have seen God do this in my life over and over again. Now I am qualified as Dr. Fiona Pyszka and have fulfilled an instruction from God that was eighteen years overdue.

The moral of the story for me is that I already missed God's instructions by eighteen years, and I was not about to miss my graduation by even a day. I was determined to graduate the year and date that I said. I was not willing to accept normal timing from the experts around me. I was willing to accept God's timing of bringing this assignment back into my life for a second chance at getting it accomplished.

Second Chances

When God gave me a second chance to fulfill a previously requested task of me, I was happy. I was happy because I got a second chance. I did not feel guilty, I felt happy. This is a key to dealing with second chances. God knows when the timing is right for you to accomplish His instructions to you. When God first wanted me to complete my doctorate, I was married for a few years and did not have any children as yet. My lifestyle was conducive to the time needed to pursue a degree. When I did not accept God's request of me, God waited before presenting it again. Why? My life changed. I had a child, we started pastoring a church and there was no proper time during this season of my life where fitting a doctoral degree would have worked.

God knows when to ask you to do an assignment. It is key for you to listen to God's instructions concerning the timing of things in your life. If you have a blind spot concerning time, you will be flustered by the lack of time to accomplish what God is asking you to do. If the fear of not having enough time is a blind spot in your life, you can overcome this fear through the process that God showed Timothy.

2 Timothy 1:7 – AMP - 7 For God did not give us a spirit of timidity or cowardice or fear, but [He has given us a spirit] of power and of love and of sound judgment and personal discipline [abilities that result in a calm, well-balanced mind and self-control].

When fear tries to enter the atmosphere of time in your life, you need to activate the Spirit of God into your time atmosphere. How? You speak out audibly that you have the Spirit of power, love and a sound mind. You speak out that you are capable of hearing and answering the voice of God. You speak out that you have all the time that God has given you to accomplish what God has asked you to do. You speak out that you have a sound mind to handle all that has to be handled with the time that you have to accomplish tasks. All of these words will change the atmosphere to allow you to be creative in your actions, and to ask God the right questions for the situation. When you operate in a sound mind you are operating in the way God created you to operate. God did not create you with a mind of failure. God created you with the ability to make sound decisions for your own life. You are capable of talking to and working with God concerning your own life. When God comes to you with a second chance, trust His timing for your life. The apostle Paul had an encounter with God that gave him a second chance.

Acts 9:5-6 – KJV - 5 And he said, Who art thou, Lord? And the Lord said, I am Jesus whom thou persecutest: it is hard for thee to kick against the pricks. 6 And he trembling and astonished said, Lord, what wilt thou have me to do? And the Lord said unto him, Arise, and go into the city, and it shall be told thee what thou must do.

Paul's acceptance of God's offer on the road to Damascus changed many lives. But most of Paul's adult life was spent persecuting the new believers of Jesus. He was pursuing legal actions against them. He was stoning them to death. He was a man hard after law and order that he perceived to be right. Paul was so wrong in his view of who Jesus was to the people of the time. Yet, God came to Paul in the time that was proper for his life. Keep in mind, Paul still had a choice to accept or reject the offer from God. Whether you are given a first chance or a second chance to do something for God, He will always ask you what you want to do. He will give you the opportunity to accept or reject His offer. The choice is always up to us. We see God show this in Deuteronomy 30:19.

Deuteronomy 30:19 – KJV - 19 I call heaven and earth to record this day against you, that I have set before you life and death, blessing and cursing: therefore choose life, that both thou and thy seed may live:

God shows us the choices we have, then He tells us which choice is better for us. He's not just showing us what we can do for Him, it's more than that because when He shows us the better choice, it is for our benefit. Whether you agree to do what God is showing you as the best option or not, does not change the fact that God will remain to be God. Your choice between life and death will not change who God is. God cannot change. He will be God now and forevermore. A blind spot the enemy uses against people is that if you give your time to God, He is robbing you in some way. Well, God cannot rob you, because He owns things you don't even know about. He has more for you than what you have now. God is trying to position us to receive what He has for us in perfect timing for us. This is why God comes and shares assignments with us, and "tells us what to do". It's because He wants us to walk in the realm of blessing He has for us. Timing is critical to these gifts God has for us.

Isaiah 64:4 - KJV - 4 For since the beginning of the world men have not heard, nor perceived by the ear, neither hath the eye seen, O God, beside thee, what he hath prepared for him that waiteth for him.

1 Corinthians 2:9 – KJV - 9 But as it is written, Eye hath not seen, nor ear heard, neither have entered into the heart of man, the things which God hath prepared for them that love him.

Whatever you age is now, whatever project you're working on and feel overwhelmed by time, stop. Stop and check your blind spots. Check to see what is pushing you into a stressed mode. Stop and ask Holy Spirit for help. Ask for a miracle if needed. But know that God has things in store for you that are based on the way He interprets time for your life and not the way the world has conditioned people to think. You can be reconditioned into God's version of time. God's timing is perfect and His timing for your life is perfect. Live confidently and be assured that God is able to do through you all that He planned for your life to accomplish. Will you give Him your lifetime to show you?

CHAPTER 6 - THINGS

When you think of things, what comes to mind? Are you thinking quantity of things? Do you think that there may be too many things? Are you thinking about not enough things? Such an interesting word, *things*. The Bible thinks it's an interesting word also. There is a well-known scripture that speaks of priority which references things.

Matthew 6:33 – KJV - 33 But seek ye first the kingdom of God, and his righteousness; and all these things shall be added unto you.

What are the things that God is talking about? If we look at the verses before, the things mentioned that people are caught up in are: the priority of who you serve (God or money), what you eat, drink, or wear. The priority of life in acquiring things is to seek God first. What does seeking God first look like? It is simple! Listen and obey. That's it. Seeking God first is all about putting God above every other person or thing. God wants to be loved first (Luke 10:27), He wants to be sought first (Matthew 6:33), and He wants to be worshiped first (Exodus 20:3). God never mandated that we not have things, His process is that we put Him first. A blind spot on things is to consider that God does not want you to have material things. The sale on such a blind spot is usually hinged on some sort of humility. The indication is that if you have too many things, you will be distracted from serving God. Well, I don't think having too many things is a problem for the people in heaven. According to the Bible, heaven's building material consists of pearls and gold. If the building material is made up of what we use for jewelry on earth, what would the items inside the buildings look like?

Revelation 21:21 – KJV - 21 And the twelve gates were twelve pearls: every several gate was of one pearl: and the street of the city was pure gold, as it were transparent glass.

The Bible also indicates that Jesus promised the disciples that in heaven He was going to prepare a place for them. What was the place going to be? Let's see.

John 14:2 KJV - 2 In my Father's house are many mansions: if it were not so, I would have told you. I go to prepare a place for you.

The will of God in heaven is not poverty or lack. Jesus' training of the disciples to pray included praying that God's will in heaven be done also on earth (Matthew 6:10). According to Jesus, it is God's will that whatever the will of the Father is in heaven, it also be on earth. Looking at the book of Genesis and the Garden of Eden, God prepared an opulent, stress free Garden for Adam and Eve to live in. God prepared this place for them on Earth. He also placed all kinds of precious stones and gold where they could see it. They did not have to "mine" for gems like we have to do now. Having nice shiny things was God's idea from the beginning. Having all provision at all times was also God's idea based on how He created the Garden to function. Then God asked Adam to do what He did in the Garden to the rest of the earth. WOW!

There are a lot of things in heaven that are without toil or don't even ware out. I wonder what that does for the worship of God in heaven. We understand that in heaven there is continual worship of God, both by the angels and by saints in heaven. How is it then, that on earth having things has become such an issue. Food, clothing, and shelter. Three things that humans use to function on earth. However, if those things are in too large of a quantity or too fancy, then there is a problem of liking those things more than God. Those lies have been sold to people as a way for them to keep pride in check. However, pride is shown in the Bible to be associated with people who disobey God. Not to people who had things in large quantity.

Romans 12:3 – AMP - 3 For by the grace [of God] given to me I say to everyone of you not to think more highly of himself [and of his importance and ability] than he ought to think; but to think so as to have sound judgment, as God has apportioned to each a degree of faith [and a purpose designed for service].

Pride is more associated with the way we think about ourselves. It is not associated with what we have. Anyone who thinks more highly of themselves than others will think this way whether they have things or not. The things do not make someone think proudly. In fact having things would reveal what type of person you are. If you are a humble person, when you have things you will be happy to share with others. If you are a proud person, you may share things with others, but want a big band to play you a song announcing just how great you are. Honoring people is not the issue, it's when you decide to honor yourself for all of your great work, that is the problem. These are the situations that point to what type of person we are.

If you have been hindering things from being added to you because you are afraid of what it will do to you, I suggest you ask Holy Spirit to help you. Ask Him to show you where you may have a character flaw that could be exploited by the devil to be used for his service and not God's. You should be thanking God that He provides more than enough for you so that you can be a blessing to those around you. You should be thanking God that what He says He will do you can partake of. This is what scripture says:

Ephesians 3:20-21 – AMP - 20 Now to Him who is able to [carry out His purpose and] do superabundantly more than all that we dare ask or think [infinitely beyond our greatest prayers, hopes, or dreams], according to His power that is at work within us, 21 to Him be the glory in the church and in Christ Jesus throughout all generations forever and ever. Amen.

If you have a blind spot of poverty, you will be opposed to a prosperous lifestyle. As a matter of fact you may even criticize such a lifestyle. In God's listing of different things that He has bestowed on people who follow Him, He never once mentioned a spirit of poverty to keep someone in check so they follow Him. Instead, we see many instances where God took people from little to plenty in one miracle. We see where Jesus provided twelve baskets more food than needed when He fed the multitude of more than five thousand (Matthew 14).

When Jesus told Peter to cast his net on the other side of the boat after Peter fished all night, Peter's catch was so much that his net broke. Peter had to call the attention of other fishermen to help him in his vast catch of fish (John 21:6). When God got involved in anything it multiplied and never decreased. The only things that decreased were things that had to do with the enemy. Demons decreased (ceased to live) in people when Jesus cast them out. Healing overflowed in people when Jesus commanded sickness to leave. All of these "things" were added to people's lives under the mighty move of God.

In the Old Testament we see that God ascribes blessings to the obedient and the disobedient receives what the curse offers. In Deuteronomy 28 there is a list of what those who obey God should expect. Nowhere in that list is there a decrease in lifestyle, ability or things. Instead, the decrease is shown in the disobedience to the things of God.

Deuteronomy 28:1-2 AMP - 28 "Now it shall be, if you diligently listen to and obey the voice of the Lord your God, being careful to do all of His commandments which I am commanding you today, the Lord your God will set you high above all the nations of the earth. 2 All these blessings will come upon you and overtake you if you pay attention to the voice of the Lord your God.

The blessing of God is promised for those who obey His commandments. The instruction is to pay attention to the voice of God. Where can we find God's voice? We find it in His Word (the Bible), we also find it in His revelation to our hearts. Depending on your maturity in your relationship with God, you can hear God's voice speak to you in your heart. People have different experiences in how they hear God's voice for their life. God can also use prophets to share with you things He would like to confirm to your life. God also uses pastors, teachers, and the five offices listed in Ephesians 4.

Ephesians 4:11-12 – AMP - 11 And [His gifts to the church were varied and] He Himself appointed some as apostles [special messengers, representatives], some as prophets [who speak a new message from God to the people], some as evangelists [who spread the good news of salvation], and some as pastors and teachers [to shepherd and guide and instruct], 12 [and He did this] to fully equip and perfect the saints (God's people) for works of service, to build up the body of Christ [the church];

The devil is your enemy, not the fivefold offices God designed to equip His people. In order for you to stay stagnant and not refreshed in your relationship with God, the enemy must deceive you. The enemy deceives people into thinking that God's offices are not for them. He deceives them into thinking that God's offices want to rob them. Here is the truth. When God creates something, the enemy tries to counterfeit those things. So, it is possible that the enemy would use an office God intended to bless His people with to rob people. But this is why we have Holy Spirit. Holy Spirit can give us discernment and show us what we should see to make proper decisions. The problem is that if you have a blind spot concerning God's blessings in your life, you will be skeptical of any opportunity or person that points you to the blessings of God. You will think there is an ulterior motive. You will think that the person is trying to deceive you out of what you have. Well, here is the way God works. If the devil succeeds in deceiving someone and causes loss in their life, God always restores them with more than what they lost. The story of Job is a perfect example of such restoration. After the devil deceived Job to fear, and robbed Job of what God had blessed him with, God restored Job. God didn't just give Job what was lost, He gave him double.

Job 42:10 – AMP - 10 The Lord restored the fortunes of Job when he prayed for his friends, and the Lord gave Job twice as much as he had before.

When young Solomon was asked by God what he wanted as a new king, Solomon asked for wisdom. God was impressed with his ask, and told him that He would also bestow riches and honor.

1 Kings 3:13 – AMP - 13 I have also given you what you have not asked, both wealth and honor, so that there will not be anyone equal to you among the kings, for all your days.

God raised Solomon to such a level during his days as king, that no one else would be higher than him. God was the one that raised him up. Did God make a mistake? Was God not aware of who Solomon was and how he was born to the woman his father had an affair with? Did God not know who He was giving all of this honor and riches to? Yes, God did know. God is in the blessing business. God does not want His children to be the tail, He wants us to be the head (See Deuteronomy 28).

Everything about God is more than enough. When God provided manna for the children of Israel in the wilderness, He provided, more than they needed. So much so, that He cautioned them not to collect for more than the day. Why? Not because He did not provide enough, it was because He was asking them to trust Him for daily bread. Besides, we know that some of them disobeyed the instructions and collected two days' worth. When people collected more than a day's worth, no one else lacked their daily needs. God does not provide in a pie chart portion. He provides more than we could ask or think (Ephesians 3:20-21).

Blind spots are things that directly affect your ability to receive from God. In your mind you will put the brakes on concerning God's provision to you. When someone wants to give you something you don't need right away, you will decline and let them know that someone else might be able to use it better than you. You never see yourself as a distributor of God's blessings, instead you see yourself as a receiver alone. Some people don't even see themselves as receivers. They only think of themselves as workers. If they don't work for what they have, then they don't deserve it. Unfortunately, they also apply this same self judgement on other people. Therefore, if someone were to share how God blessed them and they didn't "work" for what God gave them, they judge the person as lazy or unjustly receiving. However, God does not see things in this manner. The story of the midwives who obeyed God and spared babies who were slated for murder, comes to mind. The midwives obeyed God and received these blessings:

Exodus 1:20-21- KJV - 20 Therefore God dealt well with the midwives: and the people multiplied, and waxed very mighty. 21 And it came to pass, because the midwives feared God, that he made them houses.

God is a rewarder of people who seek and obey Him (Hebrews 11:6). God adds to us and He has more than enough to keep adding. God owns and creates, and He has also given us the responsibility to own and the ability to create. What else does God have to do to show us how much He loves us? He gave us His best, His Son Jesus. To think that adding anything else to us is better and higher in value than Jesus is a lie. When God gave us Jesus, He gave us His best. Nothing else He gives us will ever compare. So, if you can receive Jesus, then you can receive everything else that God has created Himself and through people on earth. No car, house, amount of money, or status on earth can compare to the magnificent riches and pricelessness of Jesus. Yet, God gave Him freely to us all. What will you do with all that God has for you? Remove any blind spots that gives you a limit to what God wants to bless you with. Your part is to obey God. Grow in hearing His voice, and accept responsibility to fulfill all His assignments to you.

Jesus is the greatest gift you can ever receive. If you

haven't already, start with Jesus. Then watch and receive all the things that God wants to add to you.

CHAPTER 7 – YOUR MOUTH

Your life is the result of what your tongue has said is possible or impossible. What?! Yes, this is what happens to us. Before you start defending yourself and give reasons for why things have happened to you, read the rest of the chapter to gain perspective. The world's system has developed processes to help people protect themselves from being accused wrongfully for things they may not have done. Why is this necessary? Because there are people who would use their tongue to speak a lie against someone else. The lie that a person speaks against another person could cause a life to be destroyed. Especially if the person spoken against is not aware that they could use their own tongue to deliver them from this evil.

If you are a born again believer of Jesus, you have an advantage over anyone in the world that is not. First, you have eternal life with God. Second, you have been authorized to use powerful words that can set your life up for major success. As a matter of fact, you can use your tongue to guide your steps. Your tongue can control your feet. In fact, the Bible puts it this way:

Proverbs 18:21- KJV - 21 Death and life are in the power of the tongue: and they that love it shall eat the fruit thereof.

Every human has been given jurisdiction of their bodies and life through their own tongue. If you are unaware of the power of your tongue, then your life has a major blind spot. Major, because you may very well be going around cursing your own life with your own tongue and blaming others. You may be blaming circumstances for your current situation but the problem could be the tool in your mouth. God gave you a tongue for you to create what you eat in life. According to Proverbs 18:21 both death and life are in the power of your tongue. The question you have to answer for your own life is, what have you been speaking about yourself?

Now, don't be alarmed if you are now realizing this fact about your life. Stop for a moment and let the light of God flood you concerning the use of your tongue for your life. The first thing you should do is stop talking about other people's lives if you are not a qualified helper to fix what they have broken. Secondly, don't allow words from other people speaking lies to remain in your presence without disqualifying them from working on you or people you lead. Now, when you do the second item, you have to be sure that your actions are not gossip. You only discuss other people's words with people you are responsible for training in the correct way. For example, as a pastor in our church I need to alert the people I'm responsible for if someone is going against the Word of God and people in the church are following their words. However, you stop at the words spoken and not pull down the character of the person. This is key in understanding how to continue being a person of godly character and still bring correction to a situation.

As a believer in Christ, you will grow in your knowledge and understanding of who you are and who

God is to you. As you grow, you must also have mercy and love for those growing around you. However, in the case of instructors of the gospel of Jesus, if they are using words to annihilate a part of the Body of Christ, you need to stop their death strikes by not participating in their actions against someone else. Participation may occur . Why? Because you are not interested in having death in your life. This is a secret and a key to a life of wellbeing. When someone is involved in gossip and backbiting, they are being deceptive towards people.

Proverbs 26:20-22 – AMP - 20 For lack of wood the fire goes out, And where there is no whisperer [who gossips], contention quiets down. 21 Like charcoal to hot embers and wood to fire, So is a contentious man to kindle strife. 22 The words of a whisperer (gossip) are like dainty morsels [to be greedily eaten]; They go down into the innermost chambers of the body [to be remembered and mused upon].

An atmosphere of contention, strife, gossip and such vile things against others is all started with the tongue. Big scandals, rumors, character assassinations, and dream killers all start with someone's tongue. Once one tongue starts a fire, even if it is a small statement, and someone else adds their tongue to the fire, then another, and another, chaos is born. People's lives have been shut down because of the tongue of another. Strife is a tool the devil uses to get his works active in an atmosphere.

James 3:16 – KJV - 16 For where envying and strife is, there is confusion and every evil work.

Do you want a peaceful environment to life in? Start with your tongue, and disqualify any envying and strife filled tongue from speaking in your ear or filling up your atmosphere. Stop the conversation mid thought and interject solutions right away. See it as putting a cloth or piece of gauze over a hemorrhaging cut and pressing hard so the blood does not run out. Be that bold and press that hard when addressing potential strife or gossiping situations. Why? Because you don't want to get the blood of the other person (the person being gossiped about) in your life or atmosphere. You want to walk away from a conversation free and clear from strife. Don't think that you can participate (silently listening and not interrupting is participating) in office gossip and go home to a peaceful house. Not so my friend. You take atmospheres with you.

Ever heard in marriages where a spouse participates in pornography and their marriage gets into trouble? Did the marriage get in trouble because the person watched pornography? Yes, but that's not the only reason. The marriage got into trouble because the atmosphere of pornography entered the marriage. When the other spouse involved in the marriage has no interest in pornography, the marriage becomes distasteful to one, while the other is just fine with such an atmosphere. What changed? Did the person watching pornography actually do the acts with someone they saw on screen? No, they participated by accepting the atmosphere of pornography into their life, and their acceptance brought the atmosphere into their marriage. Your presence in and around things matter. Why? Because your tongue will put words to the atmosphere you marinate in. Your tongue will start speaking of what you taste in the atmosphere. Still thinking that what I'm saying may not be real? Here's a story that may help you understand.

1 Samuel 17:16 – KJV - 16 And the Philistine drew near morning and evening, and presented himself forty days

In 1 Samuel 17 the story of David and Goliath is recorded. Picking up on this story we see that the Philistine (enemy) had a forty day head start on conditioning an entire army and their king before David enters the scene. While this army was marinating in the words of Goliath, David was marinating in his environment of work (shepherding) giving praise to God. Let's explore what David's environment may have looked like. We know that he was a shepherd that took care of his father's sheep. We also know from the story that he was the youngest of the family and most likely not highly esteemed. But God has a way of protecting you from drama to prepare you for the way He wants you to go. David basically spent most of his time in the field with the sheep as we see in Jesse's response to the prophet Samuel.

1 Samuel 16:11 – KJV - 11 And Samuel said unto Jesse, Are here all thy children? And he said, There remaineth yet the youngest, and, behold, he keepeth the sheep. And Samuel said unto Jesse, Send and fetch him: for we will not sit down till he come hither.

David was not invited to the family's social gathering

and was not even considered for any opportunities being offered to the children. But God knows how to find His person when He needs them. Samuel was directed by God to choose David as the next king. David was anointed for his future position and Samuel left.

After David was anointed he still continued to serve where he was before the anointing. He ministered to God and protected the sheep. He relays this information to King Saul when David had to convince Saul of his qualification to fight Goliath. But let's go back to David's environment for a moment.

For the forty days that the army and King Saul were marinating in the words of their enemy, David was giving praise and worship to God. David was killing wild animals and protecting his sheep. David was experiencing a victorious atmosphere while the army was being conditioned by their enemy. Goliath succeeded as no one was able to defeat him. But then David walked in and immediately responded from the atmosphere he came from. David spoke words that counteracted what Goliath was speaking. David questioned the mere audacity of the giant's statements and considered them defiance against God.

1 Samuel 17:26 – KJV - 26 And David spake to the men that stood by him, saying, What shall be done to the man that killeth this Philistine, and taketh away the reproach from Israel? for who is this uncircumcised Philistine, that he should defy the armies of the living God?

What was the difference between them? They both

knew the same God. They both were fighting to defend the same God. Goliath was both of their enemy. The difference to their response and success against Goliath was the atmosphere they submitted to. What areas of your life do you have a giant speaking to you? That area is becoming a bigger blind spot the more the words from the enemy gets to facilitate your thoughts. The words you permit or speak into your atmosphere will determine your win or loss in any area of life.

Take a moment and consider what area of your life is least successful. Now, examine what type of atmosphere you have created with your tongue, or accepted from another person's tongue. If you are going through life agreeing with what has been handed to you by other people's words, may I suggest you are living a mediocre life. The life God has planned for you is better than the one you accept from others. Ask God to show you the words from His Word that you should be speaking over your atmosphere. When He shows you, start speaking those words right away. Last year I wrote a book called *Self Talk Devotional*. In this book I have documented scriptures under different subject matters you should speak with your own voice into your atmosphere. You can use what I've already prepared as a start, or you can use what God has already started to show you. Either way, I urge you to get started in speaking into your atmosphere every single day. No exceptions! If you're not telling your life what to do, someone else's suggestions will prevail.

The intention of your heart is what will spill out of your mouth. If you have blind spots in your heart, those blind spots will be spoken out of your mouth into your life. The blind spots will be given the approval they need from you to be activated and used in your life. Without your permission, words cannot affect you. However, if you give permission they will do exactly what you allow them to do.

Luke 6:45 – AMP - 45 The [intrinsically] good man produces what is good and honorable and moral out of the good treasure [stored] in his heart; and the [intrinsically] evil man produces what is wicked and depraved out of the evil [in his heart]; for his mouth speaks from the overflow of his heart.

Good or bad product or fruit from your life is expressed through the mouth first. Your mouth displays the directions of your thoughts on any matter that you deem important enough to keep in your life. The things you decide are part of your character and life's mission are stored in your heart. The heart is the vault of what you consider valuable and want to take with you to the future. Your mouth displays them for you when life's decisions demand an answer from you.

Proverbs 10:19 – AMP - 19 When there are many words, transgression and offense are unavoidable, But he who controls his lips and keeps thoughtful silence is wise.

A person that speaks many words can end up being in trouble with others. However, anyone that speaks can get into trouble based on what they are speaking. The question is, are you in trouble with evil people or with those who are after God's ways? If you're in trouble with those who think and practice evil, you're in good company. Jesus was always ridiculed for being too good or doing things out of order with the traditions of men. When Jesus healed on the

Sabbath day, he was scolded by those who were more interested in upholding the traditions of men, than helping the evil work against people. People will reveal to you what they hold important through their words. You are doing the same with your words when you speak. Whether you speak many words or hardly any words, let your word be of good fruit. Don't call evil good and good evil.

Isaiah 5:20 – AMP - 20 - Woe (judgment is coming) to those who call evil good, and good evil; Who substitute darkness for light and light for darkness; Who substitute bitter for sweet and sweet for bitter!

Want to know why things may be going awry in your life? Look at what your tongue is doing. Identify who your tongue is agreeing with. Look at the belief system your tongue calls good and which belief systems your tongue calls evil. These are places to identify that may hold major blind spots concerning the use of your tongue.

Thank God for His correction and love for us. His ways are always higher than our ways. We can look to His ways and adjust our course in life. Our path on this earth can become brighter and brighter than the noonday sun.

Psalm 37:5-6 – AMP -5 Commit your way to the Lord; Trust in Him also and He will do it. 6 - He will make your righteousness [your pursuit of right standing with God] like the light,

And your judgment like [the shining

of] the noonday [sun].

God's plan for you is to shine and win. He wants you to succeed based on the plans He wrote about you. God's written plans are activated in your life, by your powerful tongue.

CHAPTER 8 - FAITH WORDS

What you say and why you are saying things carry power. The question you have to answer is, Where does the power of your words come from? Your words should produce results, especially when you are speaking solutions to problems. Results should also be seen in plans you are speaking out concerning your life. However, many times positive results are not seen and people can get discouraged. The problem with a lack of results is linked to a powerful word in the Kingdom of God, *Faith*!

Faith words carry a charge and character in them that supersedes the sounds of any other words that come from your mouth. Faith words have an origin of where they come from. Let's see where the Bible tells us that faith comes from.

Romans 10:17 – KJV - 17 So then faith cometh by hearing, and hearing by the word of God.

A blind spot against faith in your life, is to give you reasons why you don't have to read the Bible for yourself. Many Christians grow up thinking that going to church and just listening to the preacher is good enough. Well, if you want to live a mediocre life with no growth, then you are correct. Just listening to preachers without looking at the Word of God for yourself will give you vital information about God. But the problem will arise that you will not know God for yourself, you will know Him through someone else. If that someone else messes their life up, you will become messed up too. Many people walk around today with offence, hurt, trauma, and other painful experiences with church folks. Recently a surge in "church hurt" people have arisen to share their grief of being involved in messed up churches. Yup, there are such places. There are also messed up "sinning places". For example, sinners go to night clubs, bars, and any other "sinners only" environment surrounded by messed up people, and leave there with a bad taste as well. They don't like how they were treated, what they got for their money, and on and on the dissatisfaction goes.

As awful as it may be to compare these sinning spots with church, it shows a great example of how people have certain expectations that, if not met, results in offense or hurt. There is also the case where we are dealing with humans who may make a selfish decision in one second that could change the life of many people around them. This is why God wants us to build a relationship with Him, so that He can be the Rock that keeps our life together. God wants to be the only one you rely on one hundred percent. God wants to build His faith in you that can exceed the greatest faith person you know. What is the criteria of faith? You have to believe. Believe what? Believe that God is Who He said He is, and that He is capable of doing what He says He can do for YOU!

The person preaching the message may not have faith in the area of life you need faith (and they don't need to). Does that mean that you have to wait until they develop their faith in the subject before you can receive help in the matter? No. Just like offense against churches with this type of thinking, other relationships can be hindered too. For example, the relationship between husband and wife could perish because one spouse may believe more on one subject than the other. Should they wait for each other to catch up? My answer is absolutely no. As a matter of fact, use the faith you have built strength in to help in the marriage. Use the faith that you and God have developed together to accomplish what God is asking YOU to do. God's work with us is first individual before we can affect any other person. Before you can agree with your spouse or your children for something they are walking in faith for, you should have your own faith for your life. Strengthen your own faith walk so that you are a true believer of ALL that God has prepared for you as His child.

Instead of people believing by faith first for their own life by building their relationship with God, people seem to have more faith to believe God to do something for someone else. Why is this? There is a blind spot in your identity. You don't believe that you deserve what you're believing for someone else to receive. This is a blind spot. Why could you not receive the same thing as someone else? Ask yourself the question, don't bypass this accountability factor.

We see a story in the Bible where Jesus used faith concerning something having to do with Him. This is before the cross and Him believing that He will rise from the dead after burial.

Mark 11:12-14 AMP - 12 On the next day, when they had left Bethany, He was hungry. 13 Seeing at a distance a fig tree in leaf, He went to see if He would find anything on it. But He found nothing but leaves, for it was not the season for figs. 14 He said to it, "No one will ever eat fruit from you again!" And His disciples were listening [to what He said].

Jesus was hungry and went to a tree that showed leaves, indicating that fruit was present. When He did not find fruit, He shut the tree down from operating in its deception to any other person. Jesus was not angry that He did not get anything to eat. He discovered a deceiver tree and since He has dominion over trees (like we do), He took authority over the tree. Jesus used His words, but faith in what He was saying will happen. Jesus did not speak words without expecting results. His words worked for His life as well as the people who asked Him to help with their situations. The authority Jesus displayed in front of the disciples was not understood in the moment, it wasn't realized until the next day.

Mark 11:20-22 – AMP - 20 In the morning, as they were passing by, the disciples saw that the fig tree had withered away from the roots up. 21 And remembering, Peter said to Him, "Rabbi (Master), look! The fig tree which You cursed has withered!" 22 Jesus replied, "Have faith in God [constantly].

Notice the shock of Peter as he passes by the tree the next day and sees the effects of Jesus' words. Peter's response occurred after the results of the faith words that Jesus spoke were visible. At no time during the moment did Jesus look for feedback or agreement with any of the disciples to help Him speak to the tree to dry up. Jesus did not need agreement from anyone for something that He had authority over. Jesus knew this, and you should know it too. We often expect people to agree with us for things we want God to do. The bigger the "thing" is in our eyes, the more people we want to have praying with us. Now, nothing is wrong in asking for agreement in prayer. A group of people agreeing as touching anything shall be done, as the Bible tells us.

Matthew 18:19 – AMP - 19 "Again I say to you, that if two believers on earth agree [that is, are of one mind, in harmony] about anything that they ask [within the will of God], it will be done for them by My Father in heaven.

God setup a beautiful system to help His Body while they learn about Him and grow in their faith. He incorporated what I would call *the agreement principle*. How awesome that God has setup a way that you can find a prayer of agreement partner to add what they know about God on a certain subject, and what you know to secure results for a situation in God's will. This is something that allows every believer in the Body of Christ to immediately access what is available for their participation. How awesome would a new believer feel to be part of a prayer that they agreed with, and see results that they could not even imagine. Imagine being that new believer that gets to participate in miracles, and great victories. If you are a participant in a place where results like this are being secured, grab a hold of the results and grow your faith in God to have results like you'd see if you were to pray for the same thing on your own. Could you have faith to believe for such a miracle or result without the aid of another person agreeing with you? Remember that God is very much interested in a personal relationship with you. This means that He would setup more things for you and Him to do together than to always have to have someone else aide you in your relationship with Him. God wants you to believe Him for who He is to you, and not just who He is to other people. He wants you to know Him and enjoy results from Him that you pull in with your belief in Him.

Hebrews 11:6 – AMP - 6 But without faith it is impossible to [walk with God and] please Him, for whoever comes [near] to God must [necessarily] believe that God exists and that He rewards those who [earnestly and diligently] seek Him.

Pleasing God requires faith. A blind spot on faith may be that you need to be good enough to please God. But the scripture says that you please God with faith. Faith comes by hearing the Word of God. The Word of God is how we know God and it is God's revelation of Himself to mankind. Everything we know about God is written in His Word. God made things so simple for us to have access to what He can do for us, that we have to be deceived to not participate. Who is the deceiver?

Revelation 12:10 – KJV - 10 And I heard a loud voice saying in heaven, Now is come salvation, and strength, and the kingdom of our God, and the power of his Christ: for the accuser of our brethren is cast down, which accused them before our God day and night.

The devil is your enemy, and he will always be your enemy. Nothing you do will ever change his position against you. All of your energy and time on earth should be spent getting to know God deeper and better, it should not be "fighting" the devil. The tools God has given you to use against the enemy are not carnal (your physical senses), they are mighty through God.

2 Corinthians 10:3-5 KJV - 3 For though we walk in the flesh, we do not war after the flesh: 4 (For the weapons of our warfare are not carnal, but mighty through God to the pulling down of strong holds;) 5 Casting down imaginations, and every high thing that exalteth itself against the knowledge of God, and bringing into captivity every thought to the obedience of Christ;

As you can also see from this verse, the way you fight the enemy is through your mouth by faith. It's by your mouth because you are casting down (removing from a higher position than you) imaginations (pictures) and every (not one at a time), all at the same time, high thing (seen or unseen) that puts itself higher than what is true about God.

As you can see in this process of using the tools God gives you to prevent the enemy from deceiving you out of your benefits in your relationship with God, faith is required. Why faith? Because the knowledge of God is knowing about God. Knowing God is accomplished through reading about Him, talking to Him, and listening to Him speak to you. He will speak to you in your heart and in the language of His Word. This is why getting familiar with His Word is key to having knowledge of how He operates. All of this process takes faith and grows your faith. Your faith is growing because you are reading God's Word, listening to Him, hearing the fivefold offices (apostles, prophets, evangelists, pastors and teachers) and growing in your relationship with God. The more you grow in your relationship with God, the more you believe Him.

If you keep having conversations with the devil (through people that oppose the God in you), you are building a stronger relationship with your enemy than God. This is another blind spot that people miss. The blind spot is being deceived into talking with people and listening to conversations about people who are exalting themselves above the knowledge of God about you. There is a knowledge of God about who He created you to be. The Bible shows us that God already planned you and wrote who you were created to be before the foundations of the earth.

Ephesians 1:4 – KJV - 4 According as he hath chosen us in him before the foundation of the world, that we should be holy and without blame before him in love:

Psalm 139:16 – AMP - 16 - Your eyes have seen my unformed substance; and in Your book were all written

The days that were appointed for me,

When as yet there was not one of them
[even taking shape].

Growing your relationship with God should be your number one focus. To do this, build your faith using the Words God gave you, and as a bonus you will be pleasing God. How awesome is it that God has setup a system that gives us all the benefits as we grow our relationship with Him. It would be unproductive for you to spend your time listening to darkness (people who are used by the devil) describe who you are. Listening to God's view of you and reading the way He described people in the Bible, gives you great insight into what God thinks of people. Correct yourself based on what God's view of you is, not on what the devil has sent people to tell you about yourself. For example, here is just a few of the ways God sees people who put themselves under His care.

- Plans to give you an expected end. God knows where you're supposed to be at all times (Jeremiah 29:11).
- Northing can separate you from the love of God. (Romans 8:38-39).
- No weapon formed against you will prosper (Isaiah 54:17).
- No good thing will God withhold from those who walk uprightly (Psalm 84:11).

By the way, you put yourself under God's care when you have the intention in your heart to read His Word and obey what He says in His Word. For example, if God says love your neighbor as yourself (Matthew 19:19), everything about your interaction with someone that is a neighbor will be treated as you would like to be treated. Your mouth should speak words that agree with God's words about His plans for people. God wants all the world to not perish, but have everlasting life. Everlasting life can only be obtained by accepting the salvation that Jesus bought for mankind. God is interested in people helping people to find eternal life. Here is how you can help, read John 3:16 where the verse is, and put your faith in that verse. Here is how you put your faith in that verse: you read the verse and you speak out loud that you agree with all the words written there because it is what God wants. Remember faith comes by the word of God that you are hearing. If you have never led someone to Jesus, start with having faith in what God wants for all mankind.

God wants us to pass along the gift we have received to others by letting them know how they can receive for themselves. This is an example of treating others as you would like to be treated. A blind spot on being a witness for God is a huge issue for many Christians. The solution is simply to become so familiar with the gospel that you will pour out of your mouth the Words that God wrote about salvation. All you have to do is agree with God and be available to share what you know with people who don't know. Here's a verse that shows what God thinks about people who win souls for God's Kingdom:

Proverbs 11:30 – AMP -30 The fruit of the [consistently] righteous is a tree of life, And he who is wise captures and wins souls [for God—he gathers them for eternity].

Put your faith in eternal things. The first eternal thing to put faith and faith words to, is your ability to win souls to the Kingdom of God. How much confidence could you build in your life if you were to read scriptures about God's desire for mankind to have eternal life? You will have so much faith built up in you concerning God's love for mankind that it will cause you to walk in love towards mankind.

Examine yourself for a blind spot of embarrassment or feeling insecure about sharing the gospel of Jesus with people. Some of the ways a blind spot will show itself is that you feel imperfect in some way. A blind spot will have you thinking that because you are not perfect in every area of your life, what right or credibility do you have telling other people about God. Another blind spot indicator is that you think you're trying to attract people to Jesus by how well your life is going. Your life's victories are testimonies and different than the gospel. The gospel is you sharing that someone can obtain eternal life by accepting Jesus as Savior. If you meditate on the scriptures that talk about eternal life and the gospel, you will be full of faith and be convinced yourself that the person needs eternal life. The faith in you will give you what you need to share the gospel.

Take this same example of the gospel and apply it to remove any faith blind spots that you have. If you have a problem with finances, healing, friendships, a spouse, being single, being a parent, being a grandparent, a businessowner or any other position in life, find stories in the Bible and scriptures and meditate on them. Grow your knowledge on how Jesus spoke to people with problems, and grow your faith on responding like Jesus did to problems people presented. In the stories that involved Jesus, see yourself as Jesus, not the people getting the help. Your faith needs to be built in being the one that helps people instead of being the one being helped by Jesus.

John 14:12 – KJV - 12 Verily, verily, I say unto you, He that believeth on me, the works that I do shall he do also;

and greater works than these shall he do; because I go unto my Father.

If you were to just meditate on this scripture, you will find that doing things greater than Jesus did, will please God. Why? Because you will be meditating on this scripture, building your faith, and obeying something that Jesus said would happen to those who believe in Him. Just doing this one action could clear up a blind spot of inferiority about not being good enough to do great things for God. To do great things for God, you simply have to obey the Word of God that already announced you would do greater things than Jesus did.

You can remove any faith blind spot in your life by finding scriptures on the subject and meditating on them. See yourself in a position as Jesus, not as the victim being helped in the story. Having this perspective will immensely increase your faith on any subject in the Bible. Your confidence will go through the roof, you will walk in authority you were destined to have as a born again believer. You can have faith in God for ANYTHING you need on this earth.

One of the blind spots that people have is understanding the will of God for their life. God hears us when we speak according to His will. If you think that God is not hearing you, it could be that you're speaking Words that go against God's will for you.

John 5:14 – KJV -14 And this is the confidence that we have in him, that, if we ask any thing according to his will, he heareth us:

God's will is found in His Word, and it is also in the revealed instructions that He gives to you during prayer or through His prophets. Even when God speaks to you through His prophets, you will still have an inner witness about the instruction because God may have been speaking it to you already. In other words, it will bear witness with your spirit. A good example of revealed instructions to you personally would be the story of Mary, the mother of Jesus. When the angel presented God's request to her, she accepted because she knew it was God's will for HER because He asked HER.

Understand that God may ask you to do something that He has not asked anyone else to do. When this happens, the instruction from God for you to follow is His perfect will for you. Asking a lot of people if they think you should follow the instructions or if you're capable, is the opposite of having faith in God to accomplish what He said to you. When God asks you to do something, latch onto it right away with an answer of "Yes". After you say yes, provision, solutions, and directions will come to you. Mary, Elizabeth, King David, and many other people had specific requests from God for them to do. They accepted God's request and are written down in history for us to read about.

Remove any blind spots that make think that you have to be someone extraordinary to accomplish great things by faith. The qualification for accomplishing things in the Kingdom of God requires faith. Faith comes by hearing the Word of God and faith is the way to please God. You have sixty-six books with the Word of God in them to help you build faith in God for any subject matter you need on the planet earth. Get to reading and meditating on those words. Watch what happens to your life. Every blind spot will start to be flooded with light.

CHAPTER 9 – YOUR IDENTITY

A foolish person is offended by words of truth. But a wise person longs for more truth. Your identity must be secured in truth, real truth, otherwise you will end up living an insecure life. Your personal identity will be compromised and your capacity for what you were created to do will be hindered. Hence a blind spot of your proper identity will ensue. You can ruin your whole life with just this one blind spot. If you do not understand the power in which God created mankind to operate, you will settle for the mediocre crumbs of being good enough. Being good enough is a blind spot developed by the devil in the darkroom of shame and condemnation. People aim for being good enough so they can be accepted. The problem is, who are you trying to be accepted by? We see Jesus living a life on earth where acceptance was the last thing He was interested in having. Instead, He lived to do everything God wanted Him to do. As a matter of fact, He stated many times that He will only do what He sees the Father doing. Jesus was secure in His identity and what He was sent to earth to do.

John 5:19 – AMP - 19 So Jesus answered them by saying, "I assure you and most solemnly say to you, the

Son can do nothing of Himself [of His own accord], unless it is something He sees the Father doing; for whatever things the Father does, the Son [in His turn] also does in the same way.

Jesus is our example of what our identity should look like. If you are concerned that you don't know enough about God to do what He wants you to do, you don't have to be. You have the example of how Jesus did it written down in the Bible. You also have the examples of prophets and people that God moved upon in the Old Testament to do things that God would do. Thus, you can know what God would do by reading what He already did in many situations. Jesus was healing, He was casting out demons, he was raising the dead, He was cleansing the lepers. Then, Jesus told us to do the same things that He was doing. The fact that Jesus told us to do what He was doing leads us to understand what God would do.

John 14:12 – AMP - 12 I assure you and most solemnly say to you, anyone who believes in Me [as Savior] will also do the things that I do; and he will do even greater things than these [in extent and outreach], because I am going to the Father.

Once you made a decision to believe and accept Jesus as Savior, your identity becomes clearer to you because your identity of living in darkness ends. However, if you are unaware of your identity change, then you will keep behaving as if your identity never changed, only your destination after death. Many Christians think that when they receive Jesus as Savior their only benefit, for which they are thankful for, is to go to heaven someday. While this is true, you are also missing out tremendously on so much more. You are missing out on the benefit and the responsibility of owning territory for the Kingdom of God. You are missing out on using your mouth to speak a hope and a future for your life and thus you end up speaking against it.

The identity you own is created by the words you accept.

Although God has a specific identity for you, your version of your identity is based on the words you believe about yourself. Every image you see about yourself was created with words first. The pictures painted in your mind about you before you could look in the mirror, were painted by words. The question you have to ask yourself is: Where did my identity words come from? If those words about you disagree with God's authority given to you, then you need to remove those words from the painting you see. Have you ever seen a movie that portrayed how art thieves would steal and conceal expensive art pieces? They would hire an artist to paint over the original painting, so that no one would ever know that a multimillion dollar masterpiece lies beneath. Then the thief, at the right time, would wash away the beautiful fake artwork, to reveal the masterpiece. Usually the right time for the thief is when they want to use the masterpiece for their personal benefit. They would sell it or show it off for status. The devil operates the same way a thief operates. He is known as the thief, every thief gets their direction from him because he is identified by God as the thief.

John 10:10 – AMP - 10 The thief comes only in order to steal and kill and destroy. I came that they may have and enjoy life, and have it in abundance [to the full, till it overflows].

The contrast of what God has for you and what the thief wants for you are vastly different. The intention of both paint two very different pictures of who you are. What fake words (painting) has the enemy painted over the masterpiece of who God said you are? When you can identify those words, you will uncover major blind spots in your life. It may be, that uncovering these blind spots may undo all other blind spots that we've discussed so far. If you can reveal your true identity to your mind, and capture the picture of it in your heart, then the words you share with others concerning you will bring life and life more abundantly. You will no longer participate in any words that the thief had designed for you to say.

When you speak about yourself, you must believe what you are saying. If you don't believe what you are saying, then you are not speaking in faith, you are releasing words in doubt. You are literally creating doubt words into the atmosphere about yourself. Most of the time you will know you have just spoken doubt words because you will generally follow up with, "I'm just kidding". If you say something like, "Someday I'm going to be an owner of lands and businesses", and if people around you start laughing, you will follow up with "Just kidding" of "that'll be the day, huh". Maybe this is not exactly how you would demean your heart's desire in the presence of people, but maybe you've done something similar. If this is who you are now you can change your image right now. Yes, this very moment. Get in the scripture and find places where people owned land and businesses. Meditate on those scriptures and put your name in the story. Then ask Holy

Spirit for clarification on exactly where and how to acquire the tangible material related to your identity. What you own is directly attached to your identity. Don't let the devil fool you into being poor. Don't let him fool you into being the tail, his people are supposed to be the tail. You're supposed to be the head.

Deuteronomy 28:13 – AMP - 13 The Lord will make you the head (leader) and not the tail (follower); and you will be above only, and you will not be beneath, if you listen and pay attention to the commandments of the Lord your God, which I am commanding you today, to observe them carefully.

In the matters of your life, you're supposed to be the leader, not the follower. You have jurisdiction over your physical body and over your eternal future. You also have jurisdiction over what you can bring in by faith, based on what God has shown you in His Word or told you through His Rhema Word. Whether you are male, female, child, or adult, Jesus won the rights for you to have this legal jurisdiction over your own life.

Galatians 3:28 – KJV - 28 There is neither Jew nor Greek, there is neither bond nor free, there is neither male nor female: for ye are all one in Christ Jesus.

Romans 10:12 – AMP - 12 For there is no distinction between Jew and

Gentile; for the same Lord is Lord over all [of us], and [He is] abounding in riches (blessings) for all who call on Him [in faith and prayer].

Your identity as a person needs to be whole, not just so you feel better about yourself, but so that that you can participate in God's Kingdom mandate in the correct position. Consider this for a moment, when you read stories in the Bible where Jesus is healing someone, and you identify with the person being healed, your faith is being built on the fact that Jesus (or someone like Jesus is going to come heal you). But what if you read the Word and you see yourself as Jesus in the story. Even if while you're reading the story you are physically sick, you will see yourself as Jesus in the story. Once the identity of being like Jesus gets inside of you, you will not be looking for someone like Jesus to help you, instead you will heal the sick. Just like Jesus did, you will be helping people who call on you for help. You will be the one praying for the sick to recover and they will recover. You will stop doubting your ability to pray and get results, even if you yourself are sick. This is the phenomenon of faith. Why would this work if you are also sick? It will work because you are not the healer, God is the healer. You are His vessel that is yielding to operate in His Kingdom concerning healing. You are doing what you know the Father would do. You are praying for the sick, or even speaking to the sickness, and it has to listen.

Now, if you are also sick, you can believe and receive your own healing on the position of identity alone. If you think because you are sick you cannot pray healing for someone else, then you have changed your identity from being like Jesus (whole and fully healed), to being like a sick person. How can you get healing if you identify with a sick person waiting for a "Jesus" to come along and heal you? You have to start seeing yourself as a child of God (like Jesus was), capable of functioning like Jesus did to help mankind. Because you are born again, you can activate the anointing of God in you, to help others. But, if you consistently see yourself as the 'the victim' in the story, no matter who prays for you, you will never think you qualify for healing. Why? Because you think you're a victim, and victims never think they're good enough. Victims never think they deserve to be given this free gift of God's love for them.

If you live with an identity of Christ, you will be a person who walks and thinks in love. When you walk and think in love, your faith works. It will work every time for you. When you walk and think like a sick person, your love walk will be unstable. Sickness will cause you to hate yourself at times because you will start feeling condemned and ashamed that you are sick. Condemnation and shame are not qualities of love. And just like that the devil has gotten you out of the love walk with your own identity. Whoa!!!

Galatians 5:6 – KJV - 6 For in Jesus Christ neither circumcision availeth any thing, nor uncircumcision; but faith which worketh by love.

Faith works by love. If you are operating your faith with love, you will want the healing for your neighbor that you would want for yourself. This means that you just need to meditate on the Word that shows Jesus' healing operations and agree and believe that you can operate like Jesus and help your neighbor receive their healing. Understanding this, if you are sick yourself, you would want to be healed right? Well, share healing with your neighbor just like you would like for yourself that is how love works. Your faith for yourself will start working because love has been activated. You cannot activate love without giving something from yourself. For God so loved that He gave. Giving is the evidence of love. So, if you want healing yourself and you've tried everything and nothing's working, put some love in action for your neighbor with a perspective that you are like Jesus in the story of their healing. Watch what happens in your life concerning healing. Likewise, you can do the same if you want to have all sufficiency in all things?

2 Corinthians 9:8 – AMP - 8 And God is able to make all grace [every favor and earthly blessing] come in abundance to you, so that you may always [under all circumstances, regardless of the need] have complete sufficiency in everything [being completely self-sufficient in Him], and have an abundance for every good work and act of charity.

Meditate on this scripture, but also go to the Bible and read the story of someone who had this type of wealth. Solomon comes to mind. The Bible has listed all of the vast amounts of sacrifice (giving) that Solomon did for God's house. Read about the splendor of his staff and what they wore. Look at his system of getting supplies and what he ate, and what his house looked like. How about the extravagance of how he built the house of God based on God's instructions. If you were to read these stories and see yourself doing what Solomon was able to do for God, how much would your perspective of wealth change?

Remember, God gave him the riches, he didn't become a self-made billionaire. He was a God made billionaire. What about Job, God doubled Job's wealth and the story of Job includes the description of what he owned, read about the riches listed with his name. Put yourself in the story as Job and see how much your image of you and wealth will change.

If you want to please God and have faith words invade your life and your identity, you must use God's stories from His Words and create pictures of yourself this way. When you read the stories in the Bible, make sure you're identifying with the correct person. Don't be the victim in the story, be the one solving the problem. Watch what will happen in your life. WOW, you are about to go so high in faith, so rich in faith, you will be named in Hebrews 11 with the rest of the hall of faith heroes.

Can you see yourself as a story God would publish? He already published your story before you ever got here (Psalm 139:16), remember? God sees your identity as a person full of faith, He's just waiting for you to catch up with His vision of you. So, today I am exhorting you to remove your blind spots of your identity by reading and identifying with scriptures of your success and abilities in God. Start painting the image God sees of you with the Word of God, and watch the image of the enemy get washed away into the sea of forgetfulness (Ephesians 5:26; Micah 7:19, Hebrews 8:12).

CHAPTER 10 – KEEP THE WINNING VISION

The earth went through a flood where everything and everyone except those on an Ark remained, yet we still have a thriving earth to live in today. There is still the discovery of precious stones, metals, oil and other resources. Trees and animals still multiply and grow. Women are still having babies. The earth is still obeying the instructions that God gave from the beginning. The sun, moon and stars are still obeying God's instructions to them. Now it's your turn. What has your life been trained to obey from your mouth? What are you speaking to keep the vision of God's intention for your life alive on the earth?

Don't feel that if you have experienced unpleasant events in your life, you can't get back up to what God intended for you. Even though you may have had unjust events against you that traumatized you, you can overcome all of its effects by the Word of God for your life. From now on as you create vision for your life, remember to examine your thinking and eliminate blind spots that may want to limit you.

The bottom-line remedy for blind spots is to shed light on the subject. Light is shed through the words you speak.

God shows us this example in Genesis 1 when He spoke light to expose what darkness had done. You can do the same in your life. Expose the enemy's hidden agenda in you. Call out the lies he's been feeding you through your mind. Cleanse your heart's image of who you are with the Word of God. Here's a great prayer to pray concerning God's will for your life (entire prayer in Ephesians 1:17-23).

Ephesians 1:18 – AMP - 18 And [I pray] that the eyes of your heart [the very center and core of your being] may be enlightened [flooded with light by the Holy Spirit], so that you will know and cherish the hope [the divine guarantee, the confident expectation] to which He has called you, the riches of His glorious inheritance in the saints (God's people)

You can also pray this way for people for whom you have been given responsibility. Paul was praying this prayer over the church. When you pray for someone, you should pray things that you would want for yourself. Praying this way is the love principle of doing unto others what you would have them do for you.

Caution: Beware of this Blind Spot

A blind spot in the area of praying can be found in a verse that may surprise you.

Matthew 7:4-5 – KJV - 4 Or how wilt thou say to thy brother, Let me pull out the mote out of thine eye; and, behold, a beam is in thine own eye? 5 Thou hypocrite, first cast out the beam out of thine own eye; and then shalt thou see clearly to cast out the mote out of thy brother's eye.

Here is the principle. When you pray for others, don't forget to use the love principle. You would not want someone to judge you based on issues they themselves fall short in. Thus, don't have personal issues with sins that you refuse to repent for, but pray for others about those same sins as if they are the only violators in your relationship. A blind spot of defensiveness can be at play when you pray this way. Test yourself to see what you would do if someone were to point out the thing you are praying for someone about, to you. Would you be able to recognize your own sin in the area and repent, or would you be defensive (putting up protection) against what the person is saying. Defensiveness and humility do not live in the same space. If you are being defensive about something, then you have setup a barrier to correction. If you cannot be corrected, you are deemed a fool according to the Word of God.

Proverbs 9:8 – AMP -8 Do not correct a scoffer [who foolishly ridicules and takes no responsibility for his error] or he will hate you; Correct a wise man [who learns from his error], and he will love you.

Understand that this blind spot in you is something that you have to correct, don't read this passage and think of all the people who need this correction 😊 Correcting blind spots is our personal responsibility. If you look up the meaning of the word "defensive" you will find that it refers to a person who has excessive sensitivity to criticism. If you have this problem, change it by having Holy Spirit shed His light in your soul to reveal to your identity darkness that has weakened you. When darkness is present, both wisdom and light are missing. There is a scripture that you can speak as a prayer right now to ask Holy Spirit to find any defensiveness in you and remove it.

> *Psalm 139:23-24 – KJV - 23 Search me, O God, and know my heart: try me, and know my thoughts: 24 And see if there be any wicked way in me, and lead me in the way everlasting.*

This scripture will work for any other issue you may see that you have. Or you can just ask Holy Spirit to show you what may be in you that you are unaware of. Understand that when you have a revelation of a wicked thing in your life, you have to be the one to repent of it. Wickedness is not just something that you are doing that is wrong, it could be seeds that are dormant to be awakened in the right atmosphere to produce wickedness. So, preempting the enemy's plans for your life by always keeping a clean environment in your heart and soul, is the best way you can be blind spot free. A combination of the Ephesians 1 prayer and Psalm 139 prayer will set you on the right track to staying blind spot free. A blind spot is not just about having a sin issue, it is mostly about having a lack of knowledge issue. Having a lack of knowledge about your true identity, or about the things that Jesus paid for on the cross for you, is part of what could be causing blind spots in your life.

Finally

Uncovering each and every blind spot as they are planted, is a way to keep yourself clean and open to God's revelation for the next steps He wants you to take in your life. From this day forth make an effort to continually remove blind spots that the enemy is assembling in your life. Before he has a chance to bring in his darkness into your atmosphere through people or circumstances, you speak light into your life. Speak that any blind spots known or unknown from the enemy are removed far from you. Ask Holy Spirit to help you identify any situation that may hinder your personal growth. As you continue this journey of removing blind spots and living a limitless life, you now have tools to help you along the way.

You have to see yourself in positions of authority and capable of overpowering the enemy with the presence of God in your life. The atmosphere around your life should be heavy with the anointing that God has put on you and in you. When activated you defeat giants, kill pretend lions, and destroy circumstances that want to steal, kill, and destroy your life. The devil doesn't want you sick, he wants you dead. The devil doesn't want you broke, he wants you bankrupted and destroyed. The devil doesn't want people to gossip against you alone, he wants the gossip and backbiting to lead to character assassination and your name to be ruined. That's what your enemy wants for you.

What God wants is far above anything this world system has ever seen. He wants you to win battles armies could not defeat. He wants you to have treasuries full that cannot be counted. He wants you to have a life where sickness never shows up. These are things that are available to you like they were for others in the scriptures. What do you want?

What part of God's benefits for you will you accept? Do you think that you need to leave some for others? Do you feel that if you accept all God has for you that someone else will be shorted? These are not the thoughts that God has for you. According to Psalm 23, God's view of being your shepherd involves overflowing cups, green pastures, and still waters. This means provision that never dries out (green pastures), you are always overflowing with unlimited resources wherever you go (cups overflowing), and no strife in your atmosphere (still waters). All of these are benefits to you as a believer. What blind spot do you have inside of you that tells you it's pride to believe and receive all of these benefits?

Psalm 68:19 -KJV -19 Blessed be the Lord, who daily loadeth us with benefits, even the God of our salvation. Selah.

Let us all step higher and higher in the things of God. Let us accept His benefits in high levels that the earth has never seen before. Let us stop putting our hands over the cup that God is overflowing for us. Let us stop censoring God's goodness in our lives because of what people may say. God wants to extravagantly work in your life. God wants your whole household to be saved. He wants your ground to be holy and blessed. He wants you healed, complete in Him, walking confidently, with a sound mind, full of light, identity, and purpose. God wants to speak to you in ways that you understand, without it being a mystery to you. God wants all of this for you. But *what do you want?*

Examine your heart today and ask Holy Spirit to help. Find out what blind spots you've been nurturing, thinking that it is God's will. God's will is always extreme compared to the world's version of things.

Isaiah 55:8-11 – KJV - 8 For my thoughts are not your thoughts, neither are your ways my ways, saith the Lord. 9 For as the heavens are higher than the earth, so are my ways higher than your ways, and my thoughts than your thoughts. 10 For as the rain cometh down, and the snow from heaven, and returneth not thither, but watereth the earth, and maketh it bring forth and bud, that it may give seed to the sower, and bread to the eater: 11 So shall my word be that goeth forth out of my mouth: it shall not return unto me void, but it shall accomplish that which I please, and it shall prosper in the thing whereto I sent it.

Look at the richness of this passage. Can you see that barely separating yourself from the standards of the world is not part of God's will. Instead, it is God's will for a separation between the standards of God and the standards of the world to be as far apart as the heavens and earth. In other words, immeasurable. Can you remove the blind spot of measuring things you're allowed to have? Can you think in the realm of immeasurable. It's what Joseph ended up having in Egypt. The grains were so great that they could no longer be counted.

Genesis 41:49 – KJV - 49 And Joseph gathered corn as the sand of the sea, very much, until he left numbering;

for it was without number.

God's supply is always more than we could ask or think. It was God who gave Egypt the plenty of seven years. Imagine having so much supply that you have to stop numbering as described in this verse about the sand of the sea. Who created the sand and the sea? It was God who created these elements that we see right in front of us. God told Abraham the same thing about his descendants being innumerable.

Genesis 15:5-6 – KJV - 5 And he brought him forth abroad, and said, Look now toward heaven, and tell the stars, if thou be able to number them: and he said unto him, So shall thy seed be.6 And he believed in the Lord; and he counted it to him for righteousness.

Everything that is available in the Word of God, can be made real in our lives, if we believe. Abraham believed God and received what God said he could have. What has God told you about your own life? Ask Him if you haven't heard about your life from Him before. Now, whatever He says about your life, believe Him. Then, after you believe Him, follow His instructions and see what will happen. Don't pressure people to perform what God says to you for you, put "pressure" on your belief system. Break through blind spots with the Word of God, faith, and your belief in God. When you break through, move on and keep moving higher and higher into the things of God.

God designed the most amazing life for you, go live His life for you and watch what happens.

PRAYER FOR YOU

Prayer of Salvation

You can change your life by following Jesus, making Him your Lord and Savior. Man is born into sin and needs a Savior to redeem him back to God. Jesus came to take your sins and connect you back to your Father, God. He became your Savior. If you have never made Jesus the Lord of your life or accepted Him as your Savior, then this is your moment. Say this prayer with me:

Heavenly Father, in the name of Jesus, I present myself to You. I pray and ask Jesus to be Lord over my life. I confess that I am a sinner, and I need salvation. I receive Jesus as my salvation. I believe it in my heart, so I say it with my mouth: From this moment on I make Jesus the Lord over my life. Jesus, come into my heart. I believe right now that I am saved, I say it now: I am reborn. I am a Christian. I am a child of Almighty God. Amen.

Scriptures

John 3:16 For God so greatly loved and dearly prized the world that He [even] gave up His only begotten (unique) Son, so that whoever believes in (trusts in, clings to, relies on) Him shall not perish (come to destruction, be lost) but have eternal (everlasting) life.

ABOUT THE AUTHOR

Dr. Fiona Pyszka is a Personal and Professional Development Coach. Through her company, Fiona Inc., Dr. Pyszka has mentored and personally coached people from all walks of life. Her outstanding record of success in taking people from a lack of direction to focused purpose is unprecedented. Her clients fondly refer to her coaching as being "inc'd". Corporate and family units have all raved about the results they have gained through her coaching.

As a wife, mother, and ordained minister Dr. Pyszka is well aware of the demands of life on a person's entire wellbeing. Her expertise in business focuses on communication, relationship building, and leadership success. Besides the demands of her coaching business, she is also the President of Bless the Children Home, a non-profit that helps orphans and widows around the world. She has been described as a life motivator, strategist and a problem solver. Her solutions and strategies can be found in one of the more than 12 books she has authored.

Education

Dr. Fiona has earned her doctorate (Doctor of Business Administration) from Liberty University, an MBA from Regent University, and her BA in Business Administration from Lee University.

Growing Up

Raised in Guyana, South America, Dr. Pyszka knows what it is like to pursue and fulfill your purpose. She grew up as a pastor's daughter and was exposed to the many life issues her father counseled leaders and church members to overcome. Whenever her mother was not available to sit in with her father in counseling sessions, as the oldest daughter and her father's personal assistant, she would sit in the sessions. The wisdom she gained and experience she learned from within those sessions allowed her to start helping people in their life issues from an early age. She also helped to host a local radio program for the church when she was only 15 years old. Her ability to publicly speak and capture an audience was developed from this young age and these life experiences.

Now

Today, Dr. Pyszka is an international speaker and host of her own TV Program. Her most powerful and influential messages address being Fearless, Fulfilling your Purpose and Developing Strategy for Work and Life.

If you would like to schedule Dr. Pyszka at your next event, contact us at:

Fiona Inc.

P O Box 164

Palmyra, PA 17078

Or Visit: fionainc.com

If you would like to know about the amazing work Dr. Pyszka is doing with orphans in Guyana and around the world visit:

www.blessthechildrenhome.org or write to us at: P O BOX 292, Palmyra PA 17078

www.ingramcontent.com/pod-product-compliance
Lightning Source LLC
LaVergne TN
LVHW020640100826
845148LV00012B/2264